MIDNIGHT ARCADE

Magician's Gambit /
Wild Goose Chase!

by Gabe Soria
art by Kendall Hale

Penguin Workshop

DIRECTIONS

One thing you'll learn quickly here is that it's not always easy to follow the instructions. You never know when the game . . . I mean, book . . . is going to send you to your doom. But if you want a truly exhilarating experience, you'll need to do exactly what the book tells you . . . except, of course, when you get to make a choice. In these cases, you should trust your gut.

When you see a game controller like the one below, you'll be presented with multiple options to move around or take an action. Once you make a choice, turn to the corresponding page and find the matching symbol.

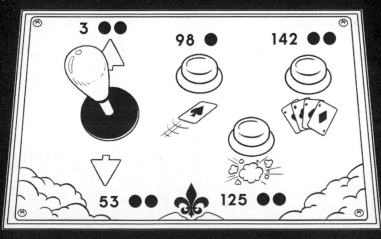

There can be as many as four sections on a page, so make sure you ONLY read the one marked with your symbol for that page.

At times, you'll be sent to a page and symbol without a choice or be presented with a chance to return to the previous stage. Do as you're instructed to keep the story flowing correctly.

Sometimes you'll make a wrong choice, and the game will end. At that time, you'll have a choice to either continue from an earlier point in the game or exit the Midnight Arcade.

There are countless ways to read this book . . . I mean, play these games . . . I mean, read this book . . . I mean . . . Well, you get the picture. Have fun, and good luck!

Welcome to the
MIDNIGHT
ARCADE

You're surrounded.

There are at least twenty of them, and they're all screaming at the same time, their voices blending into an incomprehensible cacophony that renders you unable to complete even the simplest of thoughts. They're a pack

of monsters, and they have you at their mercy. They're getting closer, closer. This is it. Prepare to die . . .

Smack! Boing! Smack, smack! The foam darts bounce off your forehead in rapid succession, and the creatures behind the projectiles disperse into the crowds of other little kids at Olde Tymes Pizza Parlour and Extreme Party Zone, the "restaurant" and entertainment complex where your little brother's birthday party (and the birthday parties of a hundred other little brothers and sisters, it seems) is taking place. Super energized by cake and ice cream and the high of opening presents, and encouraged by an assortment of padded walls, trampolines, and soft-projectile weapons, the little kids are running wild, their raised voices competing with the stereo system pumping out versions of old pop songs sung by children. It's madness, and you can't believe your parents made you come here.

"If we have to do it, so do you," said your mom.

"Just . . . be cool, okay?" said your other mom. "Have our backs on this one."

You sighed and agreed, and here you are, in what amounts to something worse than after-school detention.

You look at the table before you: half-eaten slices of "pizza," plates of cake swimming in pools of melted ice cream . . . ick. Shaking your head, you get up from the table.

"Where do you think YOU'RE sulking off to?" your mom asks.

"The restroom," you mutter, kind of lying, kind of not. Anything to get out of here for a few minutes. You love your little brother, but this is just a bit too much. You need a break.

Exiting the cavernous Extreme Party Zone, you ask one of the bored-looking teenagers who work at the place where the restroom is. They look at you like you asked them what two plus two was, roll their eyes, and jerk their thumb over their shoulder nonspecifically. O-kayyyyyy. You begin to wander in that general direction, walking down a hallway, taking a right at one corner and then a left at the next corner, and soon you find yourself kind of lost, actually. Where ARE you? Your surroundings have changed, too—the decorations have switched from the ultramodern and sporty style of the Extreme Party Zone to something more rustic, something more cowboy-like. Soon, you come to a doorway, and passing through it, you find yourself in what can only be described as "Western Saloon for Eight-Year-Olds." And then it hits you—this is the actual Olde Tymes Pizza Parlour, the chain that was bought and absorbed by the EPZ Corporation! You vaguely recall having your own birthday party here forever ago and you remember having a ton of fun. The food was good (the pizza was actually delicious, and there was fried chicken and these really great potato slices that were somehow fried and baked, soft on the inside and coated with a really tasty spice blend), and the entertainment was tops. Turning to your left, there they are: four animatronic musicians on a stage, Cats Waller and His Sarsaparilla Syncopators.

The screeching noise of something big being turned on fills the Olde Tymes Pizza Parlour, and the animatronic band comes to life, their old mechanical joints creaking as they mime playing a song energetically. And although their instruments are old-timey, the tune they're playing is decidedly not: It's an upbeat, keyboard-driven jam, a song good for aerobic exercise or . . . old-school video games. Jamming peak reached, Waller begins to sing two words, over and over:

"Midnight Arcade . . . Midnight Arcade . . ."

And then, you can hear it: the sounds of vintage arcade machines somewhere deeper in the Olde Tymes Pizza Parlour. That stirs another memory: Your moms had told you that an arcade was here when THEY were kids, and that back then it had the best games. By the time you had your birthday here, the arcade was closed. But . . . if it was closed then, how can you be hearing it now? That, combined with the jamming animatronic band . . . it's totally weird, right?

Something to the left of the stage catches your eye as the band plays: It's a doorway to another room, and over the doorway sits a neon sign that reads "Cats Waller's Backstage Game Room." That must be where the sounds are coming from! Curiosity takes hold, and passing the band—still jamming furiously, like they're actually playing—you go "backstage" and enter the game room.

What you thought was going to be a tiny room half-filled with dusty old game cabinets turns out to be the exact opposite. The game room is HUGE—from where you stand, you can't even see the far walls. Electric avenues stretch out in three directions, and right in front of you there's a change machine. Attracted by the sounds and lights, and eager not to go back to the birthday party, you take a dollar out of your pocket and feed it to the machine, looking forward to playing some games.

The machine sucks in your dollar, whirs, and then . . . spits out two coins? Two measly little gold coins? What a rip-off! You grab the tokens—they're not quarters—from the machine's tray and look down the aisle in front of you, annoyed, hoping to spot an employee and get your money back. You don't see anyone.

"Ahem!"

Spinning around, you realize that you're no longer alone. The voice you heard belongs to another teenager, but this one doesn't seem anything like the ones you ran into before. This guy is dressed like he's straight out of the early '80s, in jeans and a baseball T-shirt, with long hair and a strange look to his eyes. He stands in front of the entrance to the game room and lifts up his chin as he regards you.

"Well, all right, all right, all right," he says in approval. "Another visitor. Cool."

You hold up your tokens and begin to complain about your lost dollar, but he holds out his hands to urge you to stop.

"Whoa there, kid. Chill. You say you only got two tokens for your dollar? Well, that's all you need here at the Midnight Arcade."

When he says "Midnight Arcade," you realize that those words are emblazoned across the front of his shirt in a retro logo. You really want one. It's COOL.

"Yeah, I know," he says, seemingly responding to your unspoken desire. "We'll see. Hey, check it out." He motions with his chin that you should look behind you. You turn and realize that somehow, improbably, you're somewhere else in the vast arcade. Now you're in a cul-de-sac of cabinets, and before you are two games. On your left is a game called *Magician's Gambit*, its cabinet art promising mystery and magic centered around the exploits of what looks like a very dapper stage magician from long ago. The machine on your right is called *Wild Goose Chase!*, and its cartoony art advertises what looks like the wacky, yet criminal, exploits of a gang of farm animals and their nemesis, a hard-boiled farmer. Both of them are alight, and they both look pretty fun.

The tokens in your hand feel like they're getting warm. They want to be used.

"You're feeling it, aren't you, kid? The need to play," says the Midnight Arcade attendant at your side. "Don't fight that feeling anymore. Drop a token. Take the ride."

You approach the machines, wanting to play both, but it's time to make a choice. Which one do you want to play first?

If you want to play *Magician's Gambit*, head to 89 ●●

If you want to play *Wild Goose Chase!*, head to 205 ●●

You leap and the pin passes harmlessly and then reverses its course and flies back into Granny's hand. The ol' goose exits the car, and you and Doc follow her.

Head to 41 ●

You leap backward just as Gordo's punch sweeps the air in front of you. This thug is going to cook YOUR goose if you're not careful.

Head to 199 ● ● ● ●

● ● ●

Her rolling pin crossed with yours, Granny Goose suddenly withdraws, leaping backward as the train whips along. What's your move?

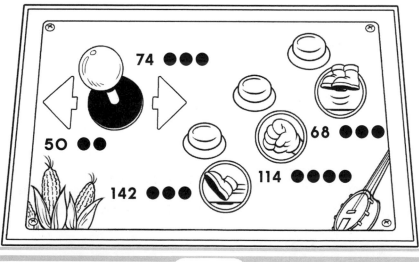

●●●●

You move forward and grab the iron gates, but they're rusted shut! You feel the vines curling around your legs, pulling you to the ground and back toward the cemetery!

YOU ARE DEAD. CONTINUE: Y/N?
Y: Head to 42 ●●   N: Head to 224 ●●

●

You hold up your hands and move your body to the left. "Nice and smooth," says Doc. "Sometimes, your opponent will telegraph where they're about to punch. Watch closely to avoid getting a glove in the kisser!"

Continue your training and head back to 57 ●●●● to try another move. If you've tried them all, head to 187 ●●●●

●●

You walk directly toward your miniature opponents, which means that they grab on to you sooner rather than later. They're fast, crawling all over you and biting and tearing and generally creating mayhem. You can't. Get. Them. Off! Soon they take you down, and . . .

YOU ARE DEAD. CONTINUE: Y/N?
Y: Head to 17 ●   N: Head to 224 ●●

●●●

You reach out and flip over the card on the right, and . . .

"Alas, a duck!" says the magician. There's a pause, in which you, Doc, and the sheriff all stare expectantly. "Well, like I said, when you pick a duck, you get nothing. This trick really could use a little work. Say, does anybody want to play a hand of rummy? It's going to be a long trip to our next stop, which I believe is in Kookamonga."

The magician deals the cards, and you, Doc, and the sheriff pick up your hands. Yes, you're about to play a card game, but as for the video game you're trapped in, it's . . .

GAME OVER
Head to 224 ●●

You walk through the lobby door on the left, expecting to enter a theater and perhaps see rows of seats descending toward a stage, but instead you find nothing but pitch-black emptiness. You don't even bump into anything, and when you feel around with your hands, you touch nothing. Wherever you've come to, it's completely empty. You cock your head in confusion, then shrug your shoulders and turn to the door you passed through, and as you do, it quickly closes, leaving you in total darkness! You whip around wildly, losing your bearings, but then suddenly a spotlight from above illuminates a space a few paces in front of you: There's a table there, on top of which is a large box that looks like a replica of a theater stage, complete with curtains drawn. As you stare at it quizzically, unseen stagehands open the curtains to reveal an empty stage. But the stage doesn't remain unoccupied for long; a marionette drops down from above, a puppet of a devil dressed in a magician's outfit. The sinister stringed being prances around the stage for a moment and then bows to you.

"Welcome," chirps the devil magician, its creepy, high-pitched voice somehow coming from its puppet mouth.

"And welcome to the final act of the show—MY show, at least!"

And then, with a flash of miniature smoke powder, it produces a deck of small playing cards in one of its tiny hands. It's such an artistic, subtle feat of puppetry that you hardly notice that no one is holding the puppet's strings.

"I hold in my hand a deck of cards," the devil puppet says, "but between you and me, this is no ordinary deck. No, these cards are special. Very special. And when you draw three cards from this deck, terrible AND great things can happen. Do you dare, magician?" You reach out to the tiny deck and draw three cards. "Be careful," the devil says, its sinister voice sending chills down your spine. "One of these cards will bring you certain death, another will bring you nothing, but one will eventually show you great wonder and bring you great delight."

Pick a card—only one—and follow its instructions!

Head to 8 ●● **Head to 48 ●●●** **Head to 47 ●●**

You lay on the horn, surprising Sheriff Farmer as he aims! He's SO surprised that he falls off the jalopy, accidentally discharging his Spud Gun into the air in the process. You slam on the brakes and reverse the car to pick him up, but he sits on the curb, despondent.

"What'd you have to go an' do that for, Deputy? Surprising me like that? I had 'em. I had 'em! And now they've gotten away. Shucks!"

THAT'S THE END, PEOPLE!
CONTINUE: Y/N?
Y: Head to 155 ●●   N: Head to 224 ●●

●●

You got . . .

. . . the Death Card!

The tiny card grows larger
in your hand until it's the
size of a normal playing card,
a card that is ice-cold to the
touch—so cold, it burns your
fingers, causing you to drop it in
pain. But the cold spreads through
your hand, up your arm, and

throughout your body, chilling you to the bone and
freezing you solid, which means . . .

YOU ARE DEAD. CONTINUE: Y/N?
Y: Head to 55 ●●●   N: Head to 224 ●●

You and Doc rush into the next car, hot on the heels of Granny Goose, and you see that you've come into a baggage car, its narrow aisle bounded on both sides by precariously stacked mountains of luggage. Near the end of the car is Granny, and she growls—GROWLS!—when she sees you. "Still after me, eh? Well then, take this!" She aims her rolling pin at you again, but this time she rolls it along the floor, as if trying to flatten you! What's your move?

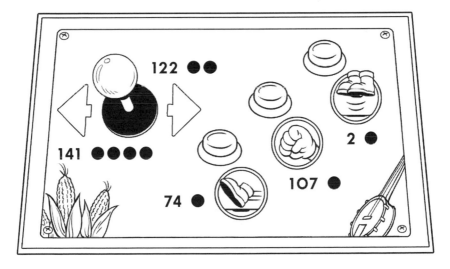

● ● ● ●

You walk back, moving to the side as Nefario's card passes by, its heat almost singeing your suit. The card flares up as it moves away and then disintegrates into nothing. That was close! But pay attention—Nefario's throwing another one! Choose again.

Head back to 79 ●

● ●

You jump into the air, and both Doc and Granny Goose look at you as if you were a goose without feathers. Choose another move!

Head back to 66 ● ● ●

●

You send a card speeding toward the mini-Nefario's card, and it cuts it in half in midair. Before the strange wooden beast can attack again, you throw another card . . . and it neatly slices the creature's neck in two, separating its head from its body! The two parts fall to the ground, and the head rolls toward you, its mouth clicking open and closed. You've beaten it!

Head to 181 ●

You dodge to the right . . . directly into the path of the flying rolling pin. You can now hear both Doc playing a mournful lament and the snickering laughter of the fleeing Granny Goose.

YOU'RE FINISHED! CONTINUE: Y/N?
Y: Head to 93 ●●●   **N: Head to 224** ●●

●●●

You've returned to the lobby. The right door is closed, but you've obtained the ticket to Nefario's finale and broken through his deadly swamp illusion. You can now go to the doors in the center or try your luck with the door on the left. What would you like to do?

If you go through the left door,
turn to 5 ●●●●

If you go to the doors in the center,
turn to 15 ●●●●

●●●●

You turn the car to the right, but the old lady sheep stops in the middle of the road, turns around, and walks directly into your path! Choose again!

Head back to 155 ●●

The rabbits advance on you rapidly, so you deploy your vanishing powder, disintegrating yourself just in time as they leap for you. When you reappear a moment later, you realize that the rabbits are now between you and your escape route down the hallway, and they're CLOSE. Before you can vanish again or draw a card, they all jump on you and make you disappear in quite a gory fashion.

YOU ARE DEAD. CONTINUE: Y/N?
Y: Head to 146 ●●● **N:** Head to 224 ●●

●●

You reach for the card in the center, turn it over, and . . . "We done got goosed!" says Doc. "Hooray!"

"But now what?" asks Sheriff Farmer. "Not much of a trick if that's all there is."

"But wait, that's not all!" announces the magician. "This trick has the flashiest finish you've ever seen. Do you feel a little . . . strange?"

At first, you have no idea what the magician is talking about, but a moment later, his meaning becomes clear—everything around you in the circus dining car is becoming hazy in a digital way, as if a screen were being slowly refreshed. The magician, Doc, and Sheriff Farmer all become pixelated and disappear, leaving you alone for a moment in digital limbo. But just as quickly as things vanished, the digital haze returns. You're being loaded back into something, but what?

Doc appears next to you, as does Sheriff Farmer, and that's when you realize where you aren't—you're no longer on the train—and where you are: You're back outside the Pig Pen! Picking the magician's Goose Card has given you a second chance to get your goose!

Head to 28 ●●●

You're in a small room, what looks to be a tiny office. In the middle of the room there is a small round table, atop of which is a crystal ball. On the other side of the table, against the wall, is another mirror, but this one is broken, its glass scattered before it, revealing what looks like the entrance to a room through the space where the intact mirror once was.

To your left and your right are two more mirrors, and behind you is the door through which you entered.

Which way will you go?

**Head to
187 ●●●**

**Head to
38 ●●●●**

**Head to
135 ●●**

● ● ● ●

You figure that the finale of Nefario's act would take place nowhere else but through the center doors, so you walk up and pull on the handles. The doors don't budge, though; they're locked tight, and no matter how hard you try to get them open, they remain shut.

"Ticket, please," drones a voice that echoes through the lobby of the theater, though you can see no one there. Ticket? Do you have one?

If you have a ticket, head to 79 ●

If you don't have a ticket, head to 55 ● ● ●

● ●

You reach for the card on the right, hesitating for a moment. Doc raises an eyebrow.

"You sure you want to go for that one, Deputy?" asks the sheriff. You shrug. One card is as good as another, you figure. You turn it over and . . .

"Well, shut my mouth and call me a guitar player," says Doc. "You got yerself the Goose Card! And you know what that means, don't cha? You get a surprise!"

"What's the surprise?" asks Sheriff Farmer.

"This," says Doc, and as he does, everything around you begins to dissolve and break into a digital blur, as if you, the sheriff, Doc, and everything on the train were made out of pixels that were losing resolution by the second. Your body feels strange, and you look around in alarm and realize that nothing is around you anymore. Everything has disappeared. You're nowhere! Or are you? For just as quickly as everything vanished, it's re-forming. But you're no longer on the train—you're back outside the Pig Pen! You found the Goose Card, and it's given you a second chance to grab your goose!

Head to 28 ●●●

You take the slip of paper with the strange word "DROWSSAP" out of your pocket and look at it. What could it mean? You say the word—"DROWSSAP, DROWSSAP, DROWSSAP . . ." Then it dawns on you: "PASSWORD!"

When you say this, the mirror cracks. Cracks again, and then again and again, until the entire surface is spider-webbed with fissures. You reach out to touch the glass, and instantly it shatters, everything falling INWARD to reveal a corridor. And running away down that corridor . . . is your miniature reflection?! Stepping through the portal, you swiftly follow, until you come to ANOTHER mirror, this one also with broken glass inside the corridor. Your reflection jumps through that mirror, and you follow right behind, drawing your cards . . . just in case.

You emerge into another, smaller room. It looks almost like a child's bedroom crossed with a toy store, for it is filled with shelves upon shelves of dolls. But upon close inspection, these aren't simply dolls—they're ventriloquist dummies! Of all shapes and sizes. The only characteristic they seem to share is that they all look like monsters, their empty eyes staring off toward a nonexistent audience in the distance. The effect is creepy, and you turn to go the way you came, but it's not there anymore! The entrance is now covered by a mirror in which you see your reflection and the reflection of the dolls behind you. *Brrrrr.*

Looking around in confusion and trying to spy a way out, you notice something else: The ventriloquist dummies aren't idle. Their eyes are tracking you as you move.

"Welcome, magician!" cries Nefario's voice, and you turn to face him, but he's not there. Well, not exactly— Tommy sits on a chair in the room, his hands and feet bound to the chair and his mouth gagged, and on his lap sits the ventriloquist dummy replica of Nefario!

The dummy's mouth begins to move, and your rival's voice emanates from its glossy wooden lips. "I'm glad to see you've followed the clues and made it this far." The Nefario dummy winks at you while Tommy struggles. "Some say that ventriloquism is a lesser art than stage magic, but I beg to differ. In fact, I find the practice of throwing one's voice to be quite an underappreciated area of entertainment. So much so that I've devoted an entire part of my act to it. But I didn't stop with throwing my voice. Oh, no. I like to put my whole BODY into it!"

The Nefario ventriloquist dummy suddenly leaps from Tommy's lap, landing on its feet in front of you. It bows and stands upright. "And what's a magician without his assistants?"

At Nefario's cue, two other dummies leap from the shelves: The first one looks like a classic vampire, and the second looks like a werewolf!

The vampire and the werewolf flank the Nefario dummy, staring at you and waiting for their master's command.

"Well," says Nefario, "what are you waiting for? There aren't any strings on you. Attack!"

The three dummies run toward you—it's time to fight magic with magic!

Nefario's dummies all leap into the air at you simultaneously, each one looking crazed and thirsty for magician's blood. What's your play?

●●

You hustle over to the right while Gordo shakes his head, clearing the cobwebs from the pummeling you gave him.

"You could've taken me right there, Deputy," he says, "but now I'm back, and I'm mad!" He puts up his dukes, ready to take you on again. *Gulp!*

Head back to 187 ●●●●

●●●

BAM! You unleash a cloud of disappearing powder at your feet, causing your body to turn intangible for a moment and move in space and time . . .

. . . directly over the gap in the stairs! You fall down into the hole and—subsequently, ironically—disappear.

YOU ARE DEAD. CONTINUE: Y/N?
Y: Head to 214 ●   **N: Head to 224** ●●

●●●●

You weave to the right, neatly evading Gordo's punch. Keep a close eye on how he moves, and you might— MIGHT—make it through this fight!

Head to 199 ●●●●

You reach out and flip over the card on the left, and . . .

"Well, you got yerself a Duck Card right there," says Doc.

"What does that mean?" you ask.

"It means that it's going to be a looooooong trip to Kookamonga," he says. And as he deals you and the sheriff hands of rummy, you know that it's . . .

GAME OVER
Head to 224 ●●

●●

You move toward the Nefario puppet, hoping to deal with it in the same manner as the vampire, but it's no dummy . . . Well, it IS, but you know what we mean. It avoids your kick and quickly throws card after card in your direction. Choose another move.

Head back to 27 ●●

●●●

Instead of fleeing down the hallway, you decide to
move toward the malevolent magical creatures . . .
and they hop on you, their razor-sharp edges and teeth
reducing you to magical ribbons almost instantly. Show's
over, magician . . .

YOU ARE DEAD. CONTINUE: Y/N?
Y: Head to 146 ●●●   N: Head to 224 ●●

●●●●

You elbow Sheriff Farmer, indicating to him that he's
got a clean shot. He fires once, twice—but misses.

"What'd you tell me to shoot for, Deputy? I ain't got a
shot, nohow! Now catch them geese!"

Choose another move!

Head back to 219 ●●●●

●

As you fall, you throw a card at Nefario, which he
dodges easily. As you descend quickly into the darkness
below the stage, the last thing you see is his triumphant
grin, and then it's . . .

GAME OVER
Head to 224 ●●

●●

You move to the left, and this moment of hesitation is all it takes for Granny Goose to take advantage of the situation by swinging her rolling pin at you and knocking you off the train! Ah, you almost had her, Deputy, but now . . .

YOU'RE FINISHED! CONTINUE: Y/N?
Y: Head to 9 ●●●   N: Head to 224 ●●

●●●

You spread your cards in a defensive motion, but the vines haven't attacked. It's like they're waiting for you to try something. Choose another move.

Head back to 35 ●●●

●●●●

Doc throws a couple of mock punches at you, and you leap back, out of reach. "Yeah, that's a good defensive move, hoppin' around like that. It won't work every time, but it should help get you out of a jam if you time it right."

Continue your training and head back to 57 ●●●● to try another move. If you've tried them all, head to 187 ●●●●

Just as Hercules is about to run into you, possibly knocking you into next week's matinee in the process, you use your vanishing powder to disappear briefly, allowing the giant rabbit to run THROUGH where you were and instead collide with the water tank! The impact finishes the work your last card throw began, and the glass continues to crack, this time even MORE violently!

Head to 151 ● ● ●

●●

You stop running and are immediately overcome by the rabbits' charge. You should have run from the rabbits' run, but instead they have run all over you, and now . . .

YOU ARE DEAD. CONTINUE: Y/N?
Y: Head to 100 ●●●   N: Head to 224 ●●

●●●

You hop around the ring, and Gordo Goose hops with you, mimicking your leaps. Soon even Doc (still playing the banjo), the rooster referee, and the audience are jumping up and down, as well. What's going on here? The whole Pig Pen is hopping, thanks to you. But seriously— how about some fighting? Choose another move.

Head back to 199 ●●●●

●●●●

You decide to keep going forward, up the stairs—if you make it across, the flames won't be able to reach you. You quickly descend a couple of steps, to get space for some momentum, and then run toward the gap! As you reach the last step, you push off and leap across the chasm, aiming for the landing . . .

Head to 110 ●

"Don't speed UP!" shouts Sheriff Farmer as you hit the gas on the jalopy, but it's too late—you're practically standing on the accelerator, and you head right into the curb, sending everybody flying. The geese have escaped!

THAT'S THE END, PEOPLE!
CONTINUE: Y/N?
Y: Head to 183 ●●   **N:** Head to 224 ●●

●●

Its two assistants out of commission, the Nefario ventriloquist dummy hisses and pulls out a deck of cards. "Never trust a dummy to do a magician's job!"

The Nefario dummy flings a card directly at you. What do you do?!

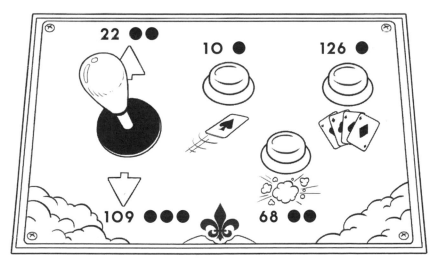

Your final punch has landed, and no, Gordo Goose is NOT getting up. You've won the boxing match and apprehended the second member of the Goose Gang! The crowd of barnyard hooligans are losing their animal minds over the upset, and the ring is being pelted with all manner of farm crops in celebration: corn, popcorn, tomatoes, poptomatoes, you get the picture.

The rooster announcer climbs back into the ring, grabs your hand and the microphone, and speaks over the noise. "Well, folks, it looks like we've got an upset on our hands and wings and hooves and paws here. Gordo Goose has been given a one-way ticket to dreamland, courtesy of our new cham-peen"—the rooster raises your arm—"KID DEPUTY!"

The crowd goes crazy again. If you've learned one thing from playing *Wild Goose Chase!*, it's that the fuzzy and feathered animal citizens of Farmingtonville LOVE a good ol'-fashioned brawl. Doc, somehow still playing his banjo, hoists you onto his shoulders, and the crowd cheers again. In a moment you've got to get back to wild-goose chasing, but for now you decide to enjoy your victory as Doc parades you out of the Pig Pen.

The cheers of the crowd at the Pig Pen are still ringing in your ears as you and Doc leave the ramshackle arena, two ringside attendants carrying the knocked-out Gordo Goose behind you on a stretcher. As soon as you exit, Sheriff Farmer drives up in the jalopy, hooting and hollering the whole time.

"We heard the fight on the radio back at the station!" he yells, throwing his hat in the air. "What a battle. What a contest of champions! I didn't think you had it in ya,

Deputy, but you sure showed me. I even lost a bet to Goober Goose over the match, if you can believe that! Money well spent, I say."

As the attendants load the still-zonked Gordo Goose into the back of the sheriff's car, he gets a serious look on his face and leans down to speak to you (and Doc). "So while we were listening to the fight, Goober Goose let slip a valuable piece of information: Seems as if Granny Goose is going to try to skip town later today on a 4:15 train out of Farmingtonville. Do you think you and Doc can get down there in time and make the arrest?"

Doc plucks a few notes on his banjo while he looks at a nonexistent wristwatch on his arm. "We'd have to really skedaddle if we want to make it, Sheriff," he says.

"Well, don't just stand there," yells the sheriff as he jumps back into his car. "Make like a watermelon and VAMOOSE!"

"You might want to offer us a ride," Doc (still playing his banjo) says laconically.

"Oh. Yeah. That makes sense." Sheriff Farmer opens the passenger-side door of the jalopy, and you and Doc pile in.

The sheriff hits the horn and skids away as you and Doc hold on.

Sheriff Farmer skids to a halt in front of Farmingtonville Station—an enormous structure that looks like a grain silo turned Gothic cathedral. You, Doc, and Sheriff Farmer jump out of the car and rush through the doors of the station and down to the tracks, where you see that there isn't just one train leaving at 4:15—there are THREE!

"All aboard!" shouts a conductor. Each of the trains' whistles blows as the engines start to chug.

Doc looks at his invisible watch. "Right on time."

"Which one do we board, Deputy?" asks Sheriff Farmer, scratching his head. "She could be on any one of those trains, and if we pick the wrong one, Granny Goose will migrate . . . to freedom!"

You spot the conductor, a sheep wearing a tidy uniform, who holds a stack of tickets in its hand. When you, Sheriff Farmer, and Doc (still playing his banjo) run

up, it holds up its arms. "Hold on, there. Tickets?"

Sheriff Farmer holds up his badge. "Farmingtonville Sheriff's Department business, Conductor. We're looking for the notorious crook Granny Goose. Did you, uh, happen to see a tough ol' goose hop on one of these?"

The sheep conductor shrugs. "I just take the tickets. You'll have to sleuth it out yourself. But you better hurry—those trains are leaving, and I can't stop 'em!"

Which train do you board?

If you board the train on the left, head to 75 ●●●●

If you board the train in the center, head to 93 ●●●

If you board the train on the right, head to 174 ●●●●

The vines suddenly whip forward, trying to wrap their mean green crushing tentacles around your body, but you disappear just in time, and they grab only empty air. Reappearing, you know you can't keep this up, so you'd better try a different move.

Head back to 42 ●●

●

POW! Your punch solidly connects with Gordo Goose's greasy goose gut, forcing the wind out of his gullet. He spins around once . . . twice . . . three times! Then he pirouettes and SWAN DIVES to the canvas. You've . . . won?!

Head to 28 ●●●

●●

You hold up the cards to your face in hopes of blocking his throw, but it slices right through your fan . . . and right through you.

GAME OVER. CONTINUE: Y/N?
Y: Head to 79 ●   N: Head to 224 ●●

● ●●

You've moved deeper into the swamp and come to
an even darker part of the path that winds through the
humid maze. You can barely see ahead; you've lost
the light! And then you see it—the swamp vines are
still creeping down the path behind you, making their
slithering, wet way toward you!

But wait. As you stare at the vines in horror, you see
something beyond them: The light has reappeared, and
this time it's BEHIND you, beyond the creepy creepers.
What's your play?

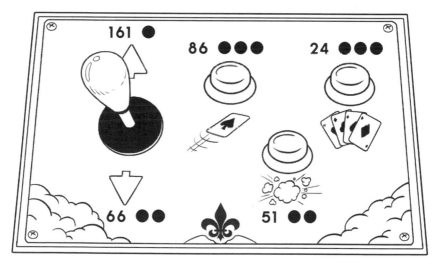

Instinctively, you unleash a volley of disappearing powder, and instead of falling through the trapdoor, you fall . . . onto the top of the coffin!

Head to 180 ●●

●

Your foot presses down on the gas pedal and you lurch forward. "Yeah, that'll give us a little bit of git-up-and-go while in pursuit," the sheriff says. "Just don't drive through a wall or into a creek or what have you."

Have you tried every control?

If not, head back to 205 ●●

If you have, head to 219 ●●●●

●●

As you exit the door on the left, it closes behind you, and you can hear it being locked by . . . something. You can't go that way anymore, so make another choice!

If you try the doors in the center,
head to 15 ●●●●

If you enter the door on the right,
head to 42 ●●

● ●

You turn the wheel to the left to swerve around the old lady sheep, but she continues to walk directly into your path. Panicking, you steer the jalopy into a lamppost on the side of the road, and with a resounding *CRASH*, you, Sheriff Farmer, and Doc are ejected from the vehicle and into the street. This goose chase is OVER.

THAT'S THE END, PEOPLE!
CONTINUE: Y/N?
Y: Head to 216 ●●   N: Head to 224 ●●

● ● ●

The evil vines approaching, you decide that the best move is to take a step back and greet them with open arms. That decision was bad, and that's the WORST move, actually. Taking advantage of your blunder, the vines spring forward quickly, wrapping themselves around your legs and pinning your arms to your torso, preventing you from performing any tricks that might help you escape. Then, the vines circle your head, and . . .

YOU ARE DEAD. CONTINUE: Y/N?
Y: Head to 42 ●●   N: Head to 224 ●●

You enter the secret room revealed behind the center mirror, and as soon as you enter, the glass of the mirror whirls up into the air, rotating like a razor-sharp tornado before refilling the gap left by its breaking. The mirror has mystically re-formed, and try as you might—kicking the mirror does nothing, nor does ramming against it with your shoulder, and throwing cards seems to have no effect on it on this side—you can't figure out how to get back through it. There must be some other way out.

Turning, you realize that you're in a small room, in the center of which is a round wooden table, and atop the table rests a crystal ball set in an ornate metal base. You raise your eyebrow in surprise—it's a mirror reflection of the room you were just in! Mist begins to fill the crystal ball. Fascinated, you step closer, and watch as the thick smoke inside the ball twists and turns in mysterious, mystic currents. Soon, though, the mist begins to clear, and a face appears in the crystal ball—the face of a devil, complete with horns and sharp fangs, looking you directly in the eye and grinning.

"Greetings," says the devil, its voice echoing from inside the crystal ball. "You've found me. Or have you? Ha ha ha!" It meets your gaze with intensity, and your

trained magician's instincts warn you that you're being lulled into a hypnotized trance. You blink, and when you open your eyes, you see that the empty space in front of the crystal ball is now occupied by three facedown playing cards! Magic is afoot in this room.

"Before you are three cards," the devil in the crystal ball says, its voice dripping with humor and menace. "One of them has the touch of death, another does nothing, but one of them contains great and wonderful magic. Try your luck! What say you, magician? Do you know when to hold them and when to fold them?"

Pick a card—only one—and follow its instructions!

Head to
213 ●●●

Head to
119 ●

Head to
185 ●

Followed by Doc, you run after Granny into the next car of the train . . . and come to a dead end! There's no way to go farther, but on either side of the car you're in, huge windows are open to the outside, through which you can see the landscape zipping by. Where's Granny?

"Kid," says Doc, playing his banjo ominously, "it looks like Granny's flown the coop on us. She's either gone out that way"—he points the headstock of the banjo to the left—"or that way"—and at that he points it to the right. "Which way should we go?"

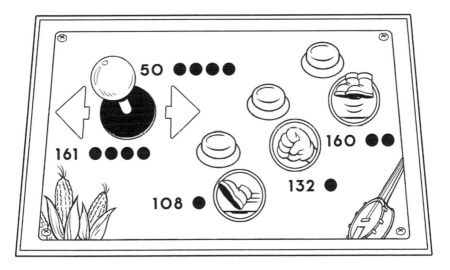

●●

You decide to investigate the open door on the right-hand side of the theater, passing over the threshold into the darkness beyond. You go farther into the murk and turn to look back at the lobby you've left behind, and as you do, the door quickly slams closed! You're trapped, wherever you are. The air around you is humid and swampy, and it feels like you're . . . outside? But how? An illusion of Nefario's, no doubt. You continue to walk forward, and as you do, your eyes adjust to the darkness while an unearthly green glow illuminates the world around you. You're on a narrow path in a decrepit, outdoor cemetery! On either side of you, crumbling tombs form an alley, behind you the path is blocked by swamp vines, and just ahead of you is a rusty gate with the words "Swamp Gate" arching over it, formed in iron letters. Beyond the gate, there's more swamp.

Contemplating your surroundings, you suddenly realize that you might not be alone . . . something behind you is MOVING! Turning, you see that the swamp vines that were blocking your path are creeping their sinuous way toward you, and even an amateur in the study of swamp vines can tell that these vines are up to no good!

You're in a dead end in a creepy cemetery of illusion.

Behind you, swamp vines with a mind of their own are moving toward you. Ahead, there's an iron gate that leads to a swamp. Make a move!

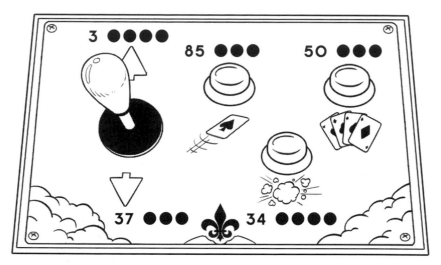

●●

You turn the steering wheel hard to the left, crashing into a row of trash cans on the side of the road, spinning out amid the debris. Steam shoots out from your car's radiator as Doc plays a lament on his banjo.

"Consarn it, Deputy," says Sheriff Farmer from inside a trash can. "We lost 'em!"

THAT'S THE END, PEOPLE!
CONTINUE: Y/N?
Y: Head to 219 ●●●●   N: Head to 224 ●●

●●●

You take a step down the hallway, headed toward the mansion's foyer and staircase, but as you walk, you notice something quite strange happening: You aren't getting any closer to your destination. In fact, once you blink, you see that the hallway has extended! You take another step . . . and the hallway lengthens even farther! You begin to run, but no matter how fast you sprint, you can't make any progress. You come to an abrupt halt and look back: You've barely moved at all. This must be one of Nefario's illusions! Choose another move.

Head back to 200 ●

●●●●

You move to meet Hercules head-on, and the bulky rabbit overcomes you with its massive rabbitness, pounding on you with its drumsticks until . . .

YOU ARE DEAD. CONTINUE: Y/N?
Y: Head to 164 ●   N: Head to 224 ●●

●●

You elbow the sheriff in the arm. "Ow!" he exclaims. "You don't have to hit me so hard. Okay, when we're driving, that'll be the signal for me to shoot when you think I've got a clear shot. Good one, Deputy. We communicate well."

Have you tried every control?
If not, head back to 205 ●●
If you have, head to 219 ●●●●

●

You rush toward Nefario just as he's about to throw his card, and your sudden, unexpected movement causes his throw to go wild. The card misses you and flies past your ear . . .

. . . into nowhere. But the distraction has bought Nefario—and his deadly magic saw—the time they both needed to complete their deadly task of sawing Professor Carter in half! You survived, but it's . . .

GAME OVER

Head to 224 ●●

●●

You selected . . .

. . . the Fool Card! The tiny jester on the card comes to life, looks at you, and laughs, then reaches out to the edges of the small card, grabbing the corners and ripping it apart from inside! In a moment, the tiny card in your hand is reduced to even tinier, almost dustlike confetti. Onstage, the puppet devil magician shrugs as someone— or someTHING—pulls its strings, drawing it back up above the stage. But still, there's no one there! *How strange*, you think as the curtains on the small stage close. A born performer, you know your cue and exit through the now-open lobby door.

If you've entered only the left door, turn to 36 ●●

If you've gone through the left and the right doors, turn to 15 ●●●●

● ● ●

You picked . . .

. . . the Devil Card!

You move your wrist in a
snapping motion, and the
card magically becomes
normal size. Another motion,
and the card disappears from
between your fingers, and
with a magician's preternatural
skills of perception, you can feel

new weight in the inside pocket of your jacket, weight
roughly equivalent to that of a high-quality playing card.
Patting that spot on your jacket, you nod at the puppet,
who bows again and then moves its puppet arm swiftly,
causing a flash of smoke and light at its feet. When the
smoke clears, the puppet has disappeared from the
stage. There is still no trace of a puppeteer.

At that, the lobby door behind you opens, and you
leave the strange mini-theater behind.

Head to 36 ● ●

●●●●

Taking advantage of Granny Goose's desperation, you figure that the best offense is, well, an offense. You swing the rolling pin and—*CLONK!*—bonk her directly on the head, causing her to spin around once, twice, three times . . . and then fall down, still clutching the bag of loot. You've done it: The final goose has been cooked! (Figuratively speaking, of course.)

Suddenly the train's brakes screech, and the entire locomotive rapidly slows, knocking you and Doc down next to the prone Granny Goose. When the train comes to a stop, you hear a voice calling you from below. Peering over the side of the train, you and Doc see Sheriff Farmer, who's rubbing a large lump on his head from where he was hit with the rolling pin. He spots you and waves.

"Howdy, Deputy. Howdy, Doc. Hope you don't mind, but I woke up from the, uh, little nap Granny Goose put me down for, and I figured that maybe I should have the train engineer, uh, stop the train so we could grab our goose. You two have any luck?"

You and Doc look at each other and then back at the sheriff. "You might say that, Sheriff," says Doc as he plays a triumphant chord on his banjo.

Head to 128 ●●●

●

You toss card after card at the vampire dummy, but each time you do, it manages to just avoid your projectile. It's a crafty puppet. Choose another move!

Head back to 131 ●●●●

●●

You feint to the left, and Granny Goose does the same. What's her strategy here? Try another move!

Head back to 2 ●●●

●●●

A vine shoots forward in an attempt to strike you, but you fan out your cards just in time to block its assault. That's not going to stop the vines from attacking again, so you'd better try something else.

Head back to 42 ●●

●●●●

You peek out of the window on the right side and look back and forth. The coast is clear, so you turn to Doc and give him a thumbs-up. It's time to see where Granny Goose has gone!

Head to 156 ●●●●

●

You rush toward the felonious fowl, but he's too quick for you, and he tosses the bomb directly on top of the police jalopy. You, Sheriff Farmer, and Doc all dive for cover as the bomb sends the jalopy to car heaven. You look up and see the Goose Gang hightailing it down the road, on their way to an easy escape.

THAT'S THE END, PEOPLE!

CONTINUE: Y/N?

Y: Head to 144 ●●   N: Head to 224 ●●

●●

Anticipating the attack of the vines, you use your vanishing powder to transport yourself away. *BOOM!* You disappear. *POOF!* You reappear . . . waist-deep in the swamp! You try to move your feet, but they're stuck firmly in the mud, and your attempts to use your vanishing powder again are stymied because the pocket it's in is now soaking wet. The mud pulls you down farther and farther and farther until the water's up to your chest, then your neck, then your chin. You manage to gasp out one last "Abracadabra" before . . .

YOU ARE DEAD. CONTINUE: Y/N?

Y: Head to 35 ●●●   N: Head to 224 ●●

In a flash, you draw card after card and, with a precise flick of the wrist, send them toward the vines, cutting them in half. But as soon as one is snipped in two, three take its place! Try another move.

Head back to 172 ●

You give Sheriff Farmer the signal, and he takes aim at the bomb with his Spud Gun and . . . *POP!* He shoots, but the potato misses its target!

"Uh-oh," says Doc as he stops playing his banjo as—

KABOOM! The bomb explodes, leaving you holding a steering wheel and not much else.

THAT'S THE END, PEOPLE!
CONTINUE: Y/N?
Y: Head to 168 ●●   **N: Head to 224** ●●

●

You quickly pull out a card and toss it at the saw, but the saw cuts right through it, slicing it neatly in half. The saw has gotten much closer to you. It's now . . .

GAME OVER. CONTINUE: Y/N?
Y: Head to 79 ●   **N: Head to 224** ●●

●●

You back away from the flying dummies only to find yourself against a wall of more puppets! The vampire and the werewolf latch on to you, and as you try to break free from their grip, you notice that the dolls on the wall behind you have come to life and are grabbing you, too. They're preventing you from accessing any of your weapons. Almost immediately you're covered in a dog pile of dummies, and . . .

YOU ARE DEAD. CONTINUE: Y/N?
Y: Head to 17 ●   N: Head to 224 ●●

●●●

There's an old lady sheep in the middle of the street and you . . . speed up? Okay, that's . . . unorthodox.

You urge the jalopy forward, and . . . *SCREECH!* You stand on the brakes just as the jalopy's about to collide with the old lady sheep, coming within inches of her. And she doesn't even notice—she keeps walking slowly across the lane, oblivious. But you've lost valuable time . . . and the Goose Gang!

THAT'S THE END, PEOPLE!
CONTINUE: Y/N?
Y: Head to 216 ●●   N: Head to 224 ●●

●●●●

You throw a card at the spot where Nefario just stood . . . and strike him as he reappears in the same place, sending him reeling backward! He kneels in pain, but he's not done . . . not yet! Keep on magic dueling!

Head to 143 ●

●

You move to the left . . . right into Gordo's punch, which knocks you in a cartwheel to the edge of the ring, where you land on your face. You try to get up, but that blow just took too much out of you. Sorry, kid, but . . .

YOU'RE KNOCKED OUT.
CONTINUE: Y/N?
Y: Head to 187 ●●●● **N: Head to 224** ●●

●●

You back away from the flames as they expand in front of you until you're up against a window on the library's far wall. Try as you might to unlatch it, the window won't budge. As the flames begin to singe a pant leg, you realize that . . .

YOU ARE DEAD. CONTINUE: Y/N?
Y: Head to 192 ● **N: Head to 224** ●●

You ascend the stairs once again and come to a landing on the third floor of the mansion. Instead of splitting into a maze of rooms and corridors, the landing stretches the width of the house, and before you is a wall with a set of two wooden doors in the center. Painted above the doors, which have beautiful brass handles, are the words "Théâtre du Monde"—it's a private theater! *Wow*, you think. It's no wonder that the professor is president of the Society of Wealthy Eccentrics—he's probably the wealthiest and most eccentric of them all.

Just outside the theater's doors, directly to the left, a beautifully painted poster advertises its next show:

The poster in the display box is lit from above by small lights, and the curious image of Nefario staring at you in a crystal ball seems to be foreshadowing the final boss battle at the end of the game. You enter the lobby and wonder how you will get to that final battle.

As if cued by your thoughts, two more doors appear and open on the theater, to the left and to the right of the main double doors in the center. Those doors, however, remain closed.

If you enter the door on the left, head to 5 ●●●●

If you approach the doors in the center, head to 15 ●●●●

If you enter the door on the right, head to 42 ●●

••••

The bomb-throwing goose is still shaking on the ground when you and Sheriff Farmer and Doc approach him.

"I was framed," squawks the goose as the sheriff puts a pair of cuffs fashioned out of corncobs around his feathery wrists.

"This character right here is Goober Goose, the third wagon wheel of the Wild Goose Gang," Sheriff Farmer tells you. "The absconding geese who took wing in different directions are Goober's flock. The big goose is his brother, Gordo Goose. He's a real bruiser, the muscle of the operation. The old bird is Granny Goose, their, uh, granny. Don't let her age fool ya, though—she's the devious brains behind the gang. She's elderly but dangerous."

You, Doc (still playing his banjo), and the sheriff walk away from the wreckage of the goose getaway car, with Goober Goose in his corncob cuffs.

"I'm going to take this miscreant to the station in downtown Farmingtonville, book him, and throw him into the ol' hoosegow—or should I say GOOSEgow?" The sheriff almost falls over laughing at his farmer dad joke, and Goober Goose takes his distraction as an opportunity to make a run for it. He doesn't even get a few steps before the sheriff recovers from his hilarity and grabs him by the collar, causing him to honk and squawk in protest. "Not so fast, you," says the sheriff.

To you, he says, "I need you to keep up the pursuit of Gordo Goose. He's the next crook you've gotta nab. But be careful—he's a brawler, a tough guy, er, goose. You might have to rough 'im up before you can take him in."

The sheriff throws Goober Goose into the back of the car and peels out, cartoon-style, headed toward the station, his prisoner squawking in protest the whole time.

"Welp," says Doc, idly picking on his banjo, "should we go after ol' Gordo?"

You nod and give Doc a thumbs-up. It's time to pluck your second bird.

You and Doc follow the trail that Gordo has left for you to follow, which isn't hard, because it's a trail of unconscious citizens of Farmingtonville, each one of them knocked out, and some with little cartoon stars circling their heads. It seems that Gordo Goose has cut a swath of cartoon destruction, all of it leading to . . .

"The Pig Pen!" Doc says with a gulp. He plays a minor-key funeral march on his banjo. "I dunno, kid. That's the roughest, toughest, meanest, most low-down-est dive in all of Farmingtonville. If you go in there, you'd better have

an extra life or two to spare, you know whut I mean?"

You nod. You certainly DO know what Doc means, but you're now a deputy of the Farmingtonville Sheriff's Department, and you've got a job to do. Hitching up your pants, you walk toward the Pig Pen, followed by a nervous-looking Doc.

You're just about to enter the doors of the Pig Pen when suddenly your way is blocked. Before you stands a mean-looking hog with a patch over one of its eyes. It snorts.

"This is a private club, kid. Members only!"

Doc strums a chord on his banjo. "Don't you know who this is? Why, this here is the pint-size perfesser of pugilism, the one and only KID DEPUTY, here to challenge the champ in the prizefights!" Doc winks at you and whispers under his breath, "We're goin' undercover, kid. Follow my lead."

The bouncer looks you up and down. "This pip-squeak is gonna challenge the CHAMP? Haw haw haw! This I gotta see. By all means, come in—the fights are already starting, and I'm sure they're waiting for you. Haw haw haw!"

The bouncer steps aside, clearing the way, and you and Doc (playing a triumphant march on his banjo) walk into the buzzing hive of farm scum and pastoral villainy called the Pig Pen.

WILD GOOSE CHASE!
LEVEL 2
GOOSETICUFFS!

Moments later, you and Doc are in a small dressing room. You've changed out of your deputy clothes into something more appropriate: satin shorts, a tank top, nifty high-top shoes, and . . . boxing gloves?!

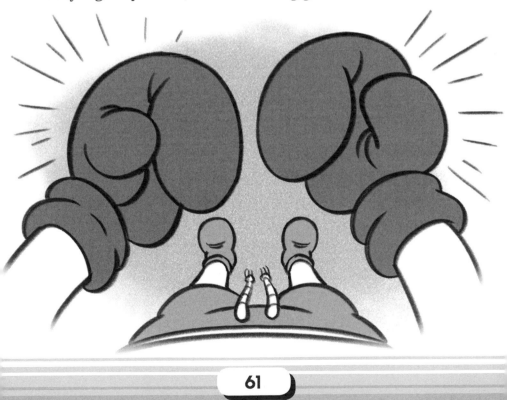

"That's right, boxing gloves," says Doc laconically. "Gordo Goose is the champ here at the Pig Pen, the top bruiser in the Featherweight Division, and you're going to have to beat him at his own game, literally, if you want to bring him to justice. Lemme see what you've got. Why don't you try out your moves?"

So, *Wild Goose Chase!* is turning into a boxing game, eh? It looks like you've got no choice but to get in the ring, so give the controls a try!

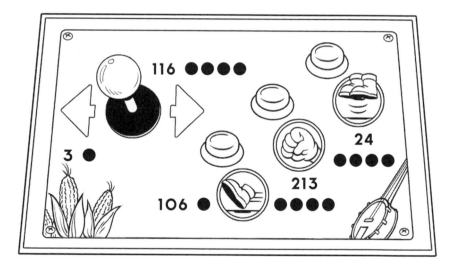

●

You spread your defensive screen of cards at the last moment, and Nefario's card is deflected away and downstage. You should go on the offensive, though, for it looks like Nefario's throwing ANOTHER card. Choose another move!

Head back to 79 ●

●●

You step on the gas and—*KERRANG!*—collide with the back of the geese's car, jolting everybody in BOTH vehicles! Your quick thinking has made them drop their bomb, though, which rolls away and blows up behind you. Keep it up, Deputy!

Head to 216 ●●

●●●

You turn your deck of cards into a fanlike shield in front of you, but you aren't being threatened by anything mystical or mundane, so it has no protective effect. Try again!

Head back to 200 ●

●●●●

You vanish just as Hercules the rabbit rushes at you, and it swipes at empty air! You reappear a moment later, and it seems as if the rabbit doesn't realize you're now behind it. Could you use this to your advantage? Hmm . . .

Head to 184 ●●●

●

You elbow Sheriff Farmer, and he waves you off. "Now isn't the time for shootin' potatoes," he says. "It's the time to drive. So drive!" Choose another move.

Head back to 216 ●●

●●

You nimbly trot forward as the vines curl around the empty space where your legs just were! They tangle around themselves, and you plunge deeper into the swamp, following the mysterious light.

Head to 35 ●●●

●●●

Instead of swerving to avoid the explosive, you swerve to collide with it. That's an odd strategy, but it certainly accomplishes one thing: It manages to blow the jalopy sky-high, along with you, Sheriff Farmer, and Doc. Your career as a deputy has come to a close, and . . .

THAT'S THE END, PEOPLE!
CONTINUE: Y/N?
Y: Head to 168 ●●   N: Head to 224 ●●

●●●●

One of the stained-glass rabbits leaps at you, and you fan your deck into a shield. The rabbit bounces off your cards—they're made from a very durable material—and lands next to its magical comrades. They hiss at you, then charge again! Move again!

Head back to 146 ●●●

●

You bounce into the air a little bit.

"C'mon, kid!" yells Gordo. "Stop yer prancin' and get to it. I'm a busy goose!"

Pick another move!

Head back to 187 ●●●●

●●

Despite it defying all logic—or perhaps BECAUSE it defies all logic, just like your magic act—you move back toward the vines . . . and they don't do anything! In fact, they vanish as you walk toward them. They're nothing but an illusion, and you walk through the ghost vines, directly to the glowing will-o'-the-wisp!

Head to 97 ●●●●

●●●

The train is still chugging along, and you're facing an increasingly desperate Granny Goose. Whatever move you make next will have to be the most decisive rolling pin decision you've ever made.

What's your move, Deputy?

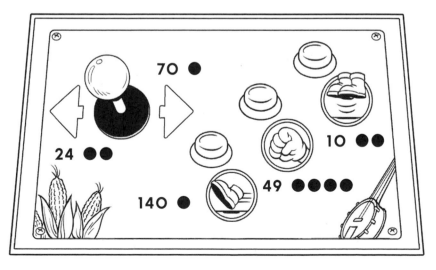

●●●●

Nefario is directly in front of you, his face fixed in a mad mask of rage and triumph, one of his cards drawn and aimed directly at you. "You've lost! Unless you've got something up your sleeve and can somehow make ME disappear, Carter will be sawed in half and I'LL be the peak prestidigitator!"

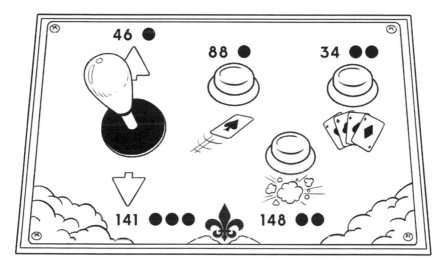

●

You elbow Sheriff Farmer, and he nods as he carefully aims his Spud Gun and fires . . . It's a direct hit on the remaining back tire of the geese's getaway vehicle, which starts to wildly weave back and forth, out of control! It spins once . . . twice . . . three times, and then comes to a stop! You've caught the Goose Gang!

Head to 144 ●●

●●

You throw a handful of flash powder that hits not only you but also your opponent. *BAM!* After the explosion, you BOTH reappear, but your positions have switched. Interesting. Perhaps you can use this maneuver again at some point, you think.

But the time to think about that is later—now you've got to kill this puppet! Choose another action.

Head back to 27 ●●

●●●

You jump up, and Granny Goose does the same. That doesn't seem to be effective at all. Try again, Deputy!

Head back to 2 ●●●

●●●●

Jumping over an ottoman on fire, you run to the door
and turn its handle . . . It's locked! With a shift of your
wrist, your personal lock-picking tools fall into your palm,
but after a moment's fiddling with the door, you know
that somehow Nefario has rigged it to be unpickable.
That's dirty pool, Nefario. Or, in this case, dirty magic.
And now you are trapped against the door as the flames
advance. It looks like . . .

YOU ARE DEAD. CONTINUE: Y/N?
Y: Head to 192 ● **N: Head to 224** ●●

●

Your leap carries you over Granny Goose's blow, but
she's prepared for that and winds up for another strike.
You'd better move again!

Head back to 156 ●●●●

●●

You manage to draw some of your remaining flash
powder from your secret pocket and quickly deploy it,
disappearing in an instant . . . and reappearing right next
to Nefario!

Head to 67 ●●●●

●●●

You jam the steering wheel to the right just as the goose throws the bomb and . . . *KA-BAM!* It explodes to your left, but you and the jalopy are unscathed! *Phew.* You pull the car back to follow the geese, but—yes, it's true—they're about to throw another bomb! Move again!

Head back to 183 ●●

●●●●

Your last card throw weakened the glass, so you figure that it can't hurt to follow up with the same move. Instantly, a card appears in your fingers. Then you bring your hand up and let it fly . . . *Smash!* The glass splinters even more!

Head to 151 ●●●

●

You move to the right, and this moment of hesitation is all it takes for Granny Goose to take advantage of the situation by swinging her rolling pin at you and knocking you off the train! Ah, you almost had her, Deputy, but now . . .

YOU'RE FINISHED! CONTINUE: Y/N?
Y: Head to 9 ●●●   N: Head to 224 ●●

You picked . . .

. . . the Fool Card, and that means you get NOTHING.
Sorry! Look at it this way: At least you didn't die.
Tossing the useless card back on the table, you exit the
way you entered, through the door that has magically
reappeared, and head to the mansion's foyer.

Head to 164 ●

●●●

You throw the wheel to the right and just narrowly avoid the bomb, which explodes as it bounces past you.

Head to 183 ●●

●●●●

You throw down a handful of your special blend of flash powder, enveloping yourself in a cloud of colored smoke, emerging from it a moment later a few feet down the hall. Nothing has changed—behind you looms the large stained-glass window. Ahead, the hallway. Pick another card, so to speak.

Head back to 200 ●

●

You figure that you might be able to get Gordo even more confused by running around him again, but the rooster referee stops you mid-run.

"That's enough of that, kid," the rooster says. "Whattaya think this is, the Farmingtonville Marathon? That's not for two weeks! Let's have a fight!"

Gordo shakes his head one last time and gets a crafty look on his face: He's recovered and ready to brawl!

Head back to 187 ●●●●

●●

You turn around and head down the hallway toward the mansion's foyer, the stained-glass rabbits clanking and scraping and hopping after you. You've bought yourself a few moments, but you'll have to deal with them eventually!

Head to 100 ●●●

●●●

You accelerate . . . and head directly into the path of the bomb! The last thing you hear before the explosion turns the jalopy into jalopy parts is the snickering of the gaggle of geese in the now-escaping car.

THAT'S THE END, PEOPLE!
CONTINUE: Y/N?
Y: Head to 168 ●●   N: Head to 224 ●●

●●●●

You bring up your fan of cards in an attempt to prevent the saw from cutting through you, but they're nowhere near as strong as you need them to be, which you find out as the saw . . . cuts the cards, so to speak.

GAME OVER. CONTINUE: Y/N?
Y: Head to 79 ●   N: Head to 224 ●●

●

You rush toward Granny Goose . . . and slip on her rolling pin as if it were a wooden banana peel! The momentum of your run, along with the cartoonlike physics of your surroundings, causes you to collide with the ceiling of the baggage car and then fall to the ground. You're in no shape to continue your hot pursuit. In fact . . .

YOU'RE FINISHED! CONTINUE: Y/N?
Y: Head to 93 ●●●   N: Head to 224 ●●

●●

You fan out your cards in front of you, and just for a moment, the approaching fire is held at bay, pushed back by a gust of wind that accompanies your flourish. But that won't hold the flames forever—choose another move!

Head to 214 ●

●●●

You move cautiously to the right, and Granny Goose does the same, blocking you from advancing. But she seems . . . a little on edge? You might be onto something here. Try something else.

Head back to 2 ●●●

●●●●

You, Sheriff Farmer, and Doc (still playing his banjo) rush over to the track on the left, running to catch up to the train as it picks up speed. A door on the train's side is still open, though, and you and your crew hop on the moving train one by one as it leaves the station. You made it! But did you make the right train?

The three of you begin to walk down the center aisle of the train, making slow progress as you stop to inspect the occasional passenger. Is this turkey a goose in disguise? Nope. How about this cow, or duck? No, not them, either. Car after car you make your inspection, turning up nothing, until you reach the engine at the front of the train.

"Nuthin'!" says Sheriff Farmer in disgust. "Shoot, and I thought we had 'er, too. Well, Deputy, two out of three ain't bad. It ain't exactly GOOD, since we let the ringleader goose get away with all the loot, but at least two members of the gang are locked up safe in the goosegow."

Sheriff Farmer scratches his head and sidles up to the train's engineer, a cheerful-looking crow with a spectacular goatee, wearing a jaunty cap and tidy overalls. "Say there, pardner. Where IS this train going, anyhoo?"

"Why, that'd be Kookamonga," says the engineer, whistling along to Doc's banjo playing. "That's just past Coconino County in about, say . . . three hundred miles as the crow flies? Or chugs along, I guess! Caw caw caw!" The crow laughs at his corny joke and pulls the train whistle. "Get it? I'm a crow and I'm not flying, I'm driving the train! Choo-choo!"

Sheriff Farmer, Doc (still playing his banjo, but now plucking it slowly and sadly), and you all slump your shoulders at the same time. "Welp," Doc says as he pulls something from his pocket and hands it to the sheriff. "I'm glad I always keep THESE on me."

Sheriff Farmer holds up the object: It's a deck of cards! "Well, I'll be. It's the Farmingtonville set of *Magician's Gambit* playing cards. 'Suitable for Gaming and Magic,' it says here on the box."

You may not have caught the final goose, but at least you've got something to divert your attention on the long way to Kookamonga.

You, Sheriff Farmer, and Doc (no longer playing his banjo; instead he's shuffling cards) dejectedly mope back a few cars from the engine, finally arriving in the lounge car of the train. You all climb into a booth, and Doc perks up a little.

"Say, y'all. Why don't we play us a little card-pickin' game? It's something Granny Doc taught me that she called Duck, Duck, Goose—I'll put out three cards, facedown, and two of 'em will be the ducks and one of 'em will be the goose. You get a Duck Card and you get nothin', but if you pick the Goose Card, you get a surprise."

"What's the surprise?" asks Sheriff Farmer.

"Well, that'd ruin the surprise, now, wouldn't it?" chuckles Doc as he performs another complicated shuffle and then deals three cards facedown in front of you and the sheriff. Which one will you pick?

Head to 22 ●   Head to 101 ●●●●   Head to 15 ●●

You hold up your ticket, and the doors ahead of you open silently. An invisible hand takes the ticket from yours and tears it in half. Without hesitating, you walk into the theater.

The houselights in the theater are up, as they would be before a performance. It's a small but sumptuously appointed place, and as you cautiously move down the center aisle, you can see that you're not alone: Tommy and Amelia are sitting in the middle of the front row! They turn and see you and attempt to call out, but their voices are muted by a ghostly musical fanfare, a riot of drums and brass signaling that the show is about to begin. The houselights dim, and all eyes turn to the stage, on which a spotlight is shining. A familiar figure slips through the curtains and stands on the stage . . . it's NEFARIO! He holds up his hands, and the music stops.

"Welcome, everyone! Welcome to the culmination of this wonderful night of mysticism and menace! It's been my honor to entertain you all evening, but what's a magic show without a grand finale? Nothing! To that end I bring you . . ."

Nefario gestures, and the curtains behind him part, revealing a coffin-like wooden cabinet floating above the floor. On one end of the cabinet, the head of Professor Carter pokes out. On the other end, his wiggling feet protrude. Nefario pulls a large hoop from the wings of the stage and moves it so the coffin passes through— there's nothing holding it up!

"Help!" Professor Carter yells in your direction. "I think this mad magician is going to use that!" His eyes turn toward the ceiling, and that's when you see it: A giant saw is suspended above the coffin, held aloft by some invisible force! Nefario bows.

"As you can see, my final trick is a bit of an oldie but goodie: I'm going to saw Professor Merlin Carter in half! Sadly, I don't know if my magical technique is good enough to put him back together. We'll just have to see, won't we? Ha ha ha ha! So face me, magician! Face me in a duel, your magic against mine. Winner takes all!"

Nefario snaps his fingers, and a spotlight shines on you

as a drumroll begins and the saw above the coffin starts to move back and forth, pushed by an unseen magical carpenter. Knowing your cue, you walk down the aisle to the stage and then mount the stairs until you're on the other side of the stage from Nefario. He pushes up one of his sleeves, then the other, revealing the lack of anything up them. Then, with a quick motion, a deck of cards appears in his hands from nowhere. It's time to have a MAGIC DUEL!

Nefario moves so swiftly, you can barely track his motion. Before you know it, he has pulled a card from his deck, and it ignites into flames as he flings it in your direction!

What's your first move?

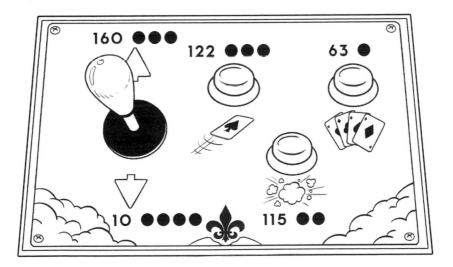

●●

You flee from Gordo's punch, and he follows you around the ring with his right fist extended, the two of you circling each other until you both get winded. The rooster referee jumps into the ring and gets between you.

"All right, all right! Enough of this jogging business," the rooster says as he holds you both at arm's length. "This is a fight, not a high-speed pursuit through the rustic lanes of Farmingtonville. I want a clean, comical fight, you hear me?"

You nod, and Gordo Goose growls. Growls! Who ever heard a goose growl? You have, and it sounds terrifying.

"Fight!" says the rooster.

Head to 199 ●●●◉

●●●

You put the strange piece of paper with the odd word "DROWSSAP" in a pocket and face the mirror. For a moment, you see only yourself, but then the mirror's surface wavers for a moment, and your reflection shifts and fades into an image of the room you were in before! You're not looking into a mirror anymore; you're looking into a portal that's inviting you to step back through it!

Head to 14 ●●●

●●●●

You lay on the horn, and it emits a cartoonish squeal, but that's it.

"Less honkin', more tonkin', Deputy," says Sheriff Farmer. "Drive!"

Choose another move.

Head back to 219 ●●●●

●

You spread a handful of cards, but they flutter away as you rapidly fall into the hole. You're a magician, after all, not a wizard who can defy the law of gravity.

GAME OVER. CONTINUE: Y/N?
Y: Head to 79 ●   **N: Head to 224** ●●

You reach for the card on the left and flip it over and . . .

"Alas, a duck!" says the magician. There's a pause, in which you, Doc, and the sheriff all stare expectantly. "Well, like I said, when you pick a duck, you get nothing. This trick really could use a little work. Say, does anybody want to play a hand of rummy? It's going to be a long trip to our next stop, which I believe is in Kookamonga."

The magician deals the cards, and you, Doc, and the sheriff pick up your hands. Yes, you're about to play a card game, but as for the video game you're trapped in, it's . . .

GAME OVER
Head to 224 ●●

●●●

You decide that your cards will be useless against the approaching vines, and you instead turn to the iron gates. They're rusted shut, but a well-thrown card should do the trick. You pull one from the deck and let it fly . . . *CHANK!* There's a flash of sparks as the card cuts through the rust, and you leap forward through the now-open gates just as the vines almost grab you. Fortunately, you're beyond their reach, but now you're IN the swamp.

Head to 172 ●

You press a button on the dashboard, and a strange contraption on your side of the car, a box with a rotating handle on it, lets out a loud wailing noise, an old-timey siren if there ever was one. Everybody in the car jumps up in cartoonish surprise.

"That's your horn, obviously. We're gonna be in hot pursuit, so you gotta use THAT to shoo any slowpoke pedestrians that might cross our path. Otherwise, we'll flatten 'em, and that's the end for us."

Have you tried every control?
If not, head back to 205 ●●
If you have, head to 219 ●●●●

●

As the green tendrils of vegetation reach toward you, you present a spread of cards to them, hoping to impede their progress. Sadly, while not intelligent, the vines know enough to go AROUND the cards, and they envelop your legs, your waist, your neck, your face . . . everything BUT your cards. And with that ironic twist . . .

YOU ARE DEAD. CONTINUE: Y/N?
Y: Head to 172 ●   N: Head to 224 ●●

●●

Hands on the wheel, you turn it to the left. Sure enough, the front wheels of the car turn to the left.

Have you tried every control?
If not, head back to 205 ●●
If you have, head to 219 ●●●●

●●●

You throw cards at the encroaching vines and notice something strange—they don't cut them at all. In fact, they seem to be passing right through them. Weird. You should probably try another move.

Head back to 35 ●●●

●●●●

Instead of throwing a mean right hook or left cross, or delivering a shattering uppercut, you begin to run around Gordo. He turns and follows you.

"You trying to make me dizzy, Deputy? I ain't that punch-drunk yet. Whyncha stop with the joggin' and get to fightin'? Or else I'm gonna have to knock you into the next game. Let's go already!"

You heard the goose—do something else!

Head back to 187 ●●●●

●

You keep running down the hall, and the rabbit falls just short of you, its glass jaws tearing a bit of fabric from your coat as it tumbles to the ground. It recovers quickly, though, and leaps at you again. Try another move!

Head back to 100 ●●●

●●

You move to the right, and Granny's swing clips you and almost knocks you off the top of the train, but you manage to hang on. But watch out—she's swinging again, so make another move!

Head back to 156 ●●●●

●●●

You draw a card and whip it toward the tank, throwing it with all of your strength . . . It buries itself deep within the glass! At first, nothing happens, and then . . . a crack appears, a splintering in the glass that multiplies, growing exponentially, until the cracks cover the surface!

Head to 154 ●

●●●●

You feint to the right, and Gordo folds his arms. "What are you doing, the fox-trot? This is a boxing match, not a dancin' marathon. Make with the punchy-punch!"

Don't make him angry—make him sorry. Choose again.

Head back to 187 ●●●●

●

In two lightning-quick motions, you draw a card and throw it, knocking the card from Nefario's hand. He yells in pain but then smirks as he looks beyond you: The saw has passed through the coffin! The audience screams and faints, and Nefario utters a gloating laugh. Your attack may have won you the battle, but it lost you the war.

GAME OVER. CONTINUE: Y/N?

Y: Head to 79 ●   **N: Head to 224** ●●

●●

The *Magician's Gambit* game calls out to you—the art on the side of the cabinet promises strange, sleight-of-hand adventures in what looks like a haunted mansion somewhere in old New Orleans, and that's right up your mystic alley. You approach the machine, studying its controls for a quick moment before you decide to pick a card from its deck of mysteries, so to speak, and drop one of your tokens into its coin slot.

When you do, a wall of curtains drops down around you and the cabinet, the kind of thing you'd see in a magic act, separating you from the rest of the Midnight Arcade! Before you can react, the room begins to spin, and your vision gets blurry. Everything around you seems to be dissolving into some sort of digital haze, and you hear a voice say, "Magician's Gambit!" You turn to see who it is, but there's nothing there except for the velvet curtain. Then, as suddenly as they came down, the curtains are raised again, and you hear applause. You also see you are no longer in the Midnight Arcade— instead, you're in what appears to be the library of a very old mansion. Books line polished shelves that reach from floor to ceiling. Spooky paintings cover the walls, and it's nighttime.

Turning around, you see that the *Magician's Gambit* machine is no longer there. Instead, there's a window that looks out on a New Orleans street. To one side, there's an empty, cold fireplace. Turning back around, you see who the applause belongs to: a trio of people, your audience, sitting on a couch in front of another window, all three of them looking at you with wonder and amazement.

"Bravo!" says one, an older gentleman wearing a three-piece suit that makes him look very rich, yet also very professorial.

"Indeed!" says another, a dashing young man who looks like he has just come from (or is just about to go to) a secret jazz club.

"Amazing!" says the third, a stylish flapper woman wearing an outfit that says she's ready to fly a biplane, drive a roadster, or hit the town all night, whichever opportunity arises first.

"What's your next trick?" asks the young woman.

Instinctually, you reach into your jacket pocket—you're wearing a snazzy tuxedo with tails—and withdraw a fancy pack of playing cards. Removing them from their box, you begin to shuffle and cut them rapidly, as if you've done this a thousand times before, like a professional magician. Cards shuffled, you return them to your pocket, close at hand if you need them.

And that's when it hits you—in this game you're a cardsharp and a magician who makes their living one trick at a time. Your audience looks at you expectantly—what's your play?

You think back to the Midnight Arcade and the controls on the *Magician's Gambit* game. Keeping them firmly in your mind, you figure that you should think of them when it's time to make a decision here in the world of the game. This seems like an ideal time to practice, what with a captive audience watching your every move.

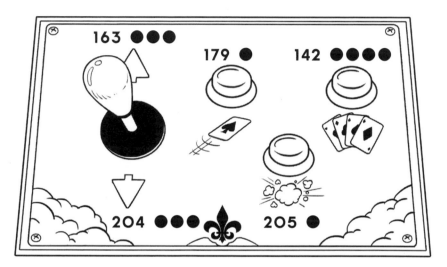

●●●

You, Doc (still playing his banjo), and Sheriff Farmer hustle straight ahead toward the train leaving on the center track. It's pulling away quickly, but you just manage to leap onto the small observation deck on the back of the train's caboose. You lean out to lend a hand to Doc and pull him up behind you, and he reaches out to grab the sheriff. Safely aboard, the three of you push open the door at the back of the caboose and enter the train.

The caboose itself is empty, but the next car is filled with an assortment of farm animals, sitting and talking and generally having a boisterous, cartoonish time. They don't notice the new passengers until Sheriff Farmer clears his throat to make an announcement.

"Ahem. 'Scuse me, y'all, but some of you might know who I am. I'm Sheriff Farmer, the head of law enforcement back there in Farmingtonville. Me and my posse here"—he holds out an open palm to indicate you and Doc, who's playing a quiet little progression of notes on his banjo—"have boarded this train in pursuit of a wanted criminal." A murmur goes through the seated passengers. "Yes, that's right. We have reason to believe that Granny Goose of the Wild Goose Gang is hiding somewhere on this train, and we'd like to know if anyone's seen anything . . . suspicious."

Sheriff Farmer walks down the aisle, turning his head from side to side, looking at the passengers closely. "Granny's trail has led us to this train, and I'm sure all of you are familiar with her and her boys' exploits. The latest caper they pulled was a bank robbery in downtown Farmingtonville earlier today that netted them a whole lotta moola. My deputy here has proved instrumental in apprehending the other suspects in a high-speed chase and then a boxing match, if you can believe it. Can you believe it?"

The passengers murmur again, looking at you with amusement and respect, while the sheriff continues down the aisle. "Anyway, we'd sure like to get to the bottom of this case and close it all up before suppertime. I hear there's apple pie for dessert tonight at home, and you know that I love me some apple pie. Mmm-mm! Hey . . ."

The sheriff's eye is caught by something on the ground, and he kneels to pick it up. "What's this? Hey—it's money! Say, ma'am, I believe you dropped something." He stands and holds the bill out to the animal in the seat next to him, who snatches it back quickly. The animal's dressed in sunglasses and a scarf, and is holding a large bag. A large bag that seems to be leaking . . . money! You clear your throat to bring it to the sheriff's attention, and in a flash of movement, the passenger whips off her sunglasses and scarf to reveal her true identity—it's Granny Goose! And she's wielding a massive rolling pin in a VERY threatening manner. Clutching her bag of money closely, she backs down the aisle, away from the sheriff.

"You may have nabbed my boys, but this is one goose that's too slippery for the likes of you, Sheriff!"

"Now, now, Granny," says Sheriff Farmer. "Just hand over the money and come along quietly, and we can all have some apple pie down at the station. What d'ya say? We outnumber you."

Granny Goose pauses for a moment, her beady goose eyes moving from the sheriff to you and back to the sheriff. "I say . . ."

WHOOP! Granny throws her rolling pin, clonking the sheriff directly in the middle of the forehead and knocking him flat on his back. Bizarrely, the rolling pin returns to her hand, whizzing back as if it were a boomerang.

"Ha! That evens the odds, doesn't it? Haw haw haw! And now who's going to stop me? YOU?" She points the rolling pin at you threateningly. "I don't care what you did to my boys; if you think Granny Goose is going to be nabbed by any pip-squeak deputy, then, well . . ." Granny pauses for a second, thinking. Finally, her mean old eyes brighten. "Well then, you can think again!"

Granny brings her arm back . . . and throws the rolling pin straight at you! What's your move?

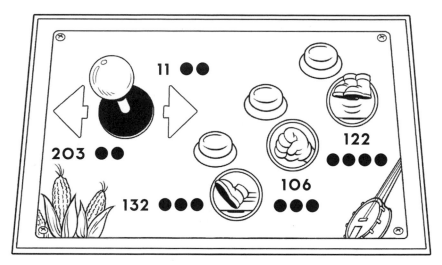

●●●●

You step forward, drawing closer to the bouncing light. The sounds of the swamp get louder and louder as you reach toward the floating, glowing globe, finally enveloping it in your hand. Its glow shines through your fingers for a moment, and it feels warm, but the light and the sensation of heat fade quickly. Opening your hand, you see that the light is gone, and you're holding . . . a ticket! The swamp around you begins to melt away, and in the blink of an eye, you're back in the theater lobby on the third floor of the mansion. So the swamp WAS just an illusion! But the piece of paper you're holding is no magic trick. It's as real as your deck of cards.

YOU GOT . . .

THE TICKET TO THE FINALE!

If you've only gone through the right door, head to 11 ●●●

If you've gone through the right door and the left door, head to 15 ●●●●

●

You aim a card toward the flying puppets, and it finds its home directly between the eyes of the werewolf! It falls to the floor, dead. Or as dead as a ventriloquist dummy can be.

Head to 131 ●●●●

●●

You pull the jalopy over to the left, trying to outflank the getaway geese, but that move only puts you in the path of the next bomb. *KABLOOEY!* You've been smithereened!

THAT'S THE END, PEOPLE!
CONTINUE: Y/N?
Y: Head to 183 ●●   **N: Head to 224** ●●

●●●

Even though there's nothing to defend against, you spread your card shield. Great. But in magic, timing is everything—and your timing this time is really lacking, for while you are posing, Nefario has appeared behind you! Turning, you see him smile just before he disappears again. Choose another move!

Head back to 127 ●●

●●●●

You slowly move to the right, your fists dancing in front of you. Gordo does the exact opposite and moves to the left, keeping close to you but not TOO close. You're going to have to get him some other way.

Head back to 199 ●●●●

●

You decide that you want to get a closer look at the strange stained-glass window before you explore the rest of the mansion, so you turn around and go down the hall to the bizarre, colorful, and intricate work of art.

Head to 146 ●●●

●●

You jam the steering wheel to the left just as Sheriff Farmer aims to shoot out another tire on the geese's getaway car, and he almost falls off the side of the jalopy.

"Keep it steady, Deputy, or else we'll never get these crooks!" Try another move.

Head back to 153 ●●●●

●●●

You're running down the hallway leading to the house's foyer, the clinking of the stained-glass rabbits right behind you. You hazard a glance over your shoulder and see that the lead rabbit is leaping into the air and launching itself right at you!

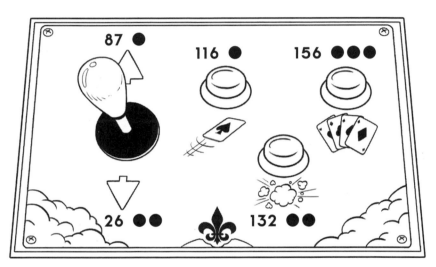

●●●●

You reach for the card in the middle and flip it over, and . . .

. . . you got a Duck Card! Rats! Or ducks. You know what we mean.

"Aw, shoot," says Sheriff Farmer, snatching his hat from his head and throwing it in disgust. "I wanted to see what that Goose Card did."

"I did, too," replies Doc, shaking his head and collecting all the cards together. He begins shuffling them again. "But now that that's over, who's up for a round of Coconino County Poker?"

The sheriff raises his hand, and Doc begins dealing, and even though you don't know how to play, you figure that you'll have plenty of time to learn, since now it's . . .

GAME OVER
Head to 224 ●●

You selected . . .

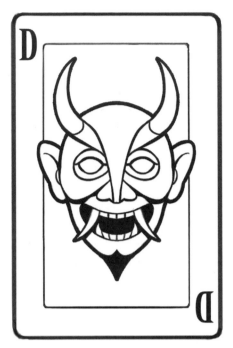

. . . the Devil Card! And while to the eye it appears to be nothing more than a high-quality playing card, it feels warm in your hand, as if there's something ALIVE inside it. WEIRD. Slipping the card into the pocket on the inside of your jacket, you turn away from the strange dealer at the table and exit the room through the door that has reappeared, hastening to the foyer of the mansion.

Head to 164 ●

●●

You duck out of the way of the bomb by leaping to the right, but the bomb blows up in front of you, Sheriff Farmer, and Doc, sending all of you scrambling for cover behind the jalopy. When you peek over the car's hood, the Goose Gang has vanished!

"Dagnabbit," says Sheriff Farmer, throwing his hat on the ground and stomping on it. "All that farm police work . . . for nuthin'. Phooey!"

THAT'S THE END, PEOPLE!
CONTINUE: Y/N ?
Y: Head to 153 ●●●●   N: Head to 224 ●●

●●●

Taking the piece of paper that reads "ENO TCA" from the table, you hear Nefario's laughter all around you. "Not good, but not bad, either. It seems like you might need a little bit more experience to face me."

As Nefario laughs again, a mist begins to fill the room. All is obscured, and you try to feel your way around. Your hand touches something! The mist clears, and you see you're back in the library at the beginning of the game.

NEFARIO!!!

Head to 192 ●

●●●●

You pull the single Devil Card you obtained in the mansion from your pocket and hold it up, observing the strange illustration on it and admiring the craftsmanship of the card. Suddenly the card ignites! Flames engulf the paper, and you toss it away from you as the heat burns your fingers. The card falls to the stage, where it crumples and folds in on itself, turning to ash as the flames die. Soon, all that's left of the card is a pile of burnt paper on the ground. You look at the audience, and they look back at you, disappointment barely hidden on their faces.

But then, something begins to happen to the small pile of ashes. The remains begin to shift, as if there's something buried beneath them trying to free itself. What that thing is reveals itself moments later as two skeletal hands push out from the debris, hands attached to skeletal arms, followed by a skeletal head, and then an entire skeleton body! It's only six inches tall, but from what you can see, it's REAL. The small skeleton kicks the ashes away from its feet and looks around, spotting you and the audience watching it. It bows to you, then to the audience, and then begins to do a funny, shuffling dance, leaping to and fro on the stage, taking its head off and throwing it up into the air only to catch it on its way down . . . It's a charming, weird little performance that winds down moments later when the skeleton returns to the pile of card ashes, digs itself back into them, and then neatly covers up its grave with its skeletal hands before pulling them in, too. Immediately after it reburies itself, a breeze blows through the theater and scatters the ashes, underneath which there's . . . nothing. The skeleton's GONE!

The enraptured audience members are silent for a moment and then begin to clap appreciatively, impressed with the strange, magical display they've just seen. You take a bow, and as you do, a mist begins to creep around your legs, slowly getting thicker and thicker until you can no longer see the audience or even the stage around you! The theater has disappeared, the applause becoming fainter and fainter as another sound replaces it: the sound of arcade games! As the smoke clears, you can see that you're no longer inside *Magician's Gambit*—you've returned to your own world!

If you want to play *Wild Goose Chase!*, turn to 205 ●●

If you've completed both games, turn to 224 ●●

●

You make a quick circle around Doc, doing your best to make him dizzy, it seems. "That's a good one," he says. "You wanna try that move when you need to razzle-dazzle and confuse yer opponent."

Continue your training and head back to 57 ●●●● to try another move. If you've tried them all, head to 187 ●●●●

●●

Figuring one good disappearing act deserves another, you unleash your flash powder, as well. *Poof!* When you reappear, you and Nefario are at the opposite ends of the stage, ready to face off again!

Head back to 79 ●

●●●

You don't have anything to attack with. Try another move.

Head back to 93 ●●●

●●●●

There's nothing to block here with your admittedly very cool-looking card-fanning move, and if you don't do something else quickly, both you and Amelia will be done for. Try something else!

Head back to 184 ●●●

●

You don't have any sort of weapon to fight with. Choose another move, but choose quickly!

Head back to 9 ●●●

●●

You fan out your cards and use them as a shield when a tongue of flames reaches out toward your face. It deflects the fire and provides a slight respite from the heat when you wave it in front of your face, but you need to get out of here. Move again, and make it snappy!

Head back to 192 ●

● ● ●

You give Sheriff Farmer the signal, and he pokes his tongue out the corner of his mouth, takes careful aim, and . . . *POW!* His potato projectile strikes one of the back tires of the goosemobile and blows it up! The car wobbles a bit, but it's still running. You'll have to get them at least one more time before you bring the car to a halt.

Head to 216 ● ●

● ● ● ●

How did Nefario get out of here? That's right—he vanished! That's the secret to pulling off this escape. Vanishing! With a gesture, you throw your special mix of flash powder at the ground, and it envelops you in a column of light and smoke. A second later, it clears, and you're now in a hallway outside the library. Pretty magical.

Head to 200 ●

●

Where are you going to run to, Deputy? Choose a window to go through!

Head back to 41 ●

●●

You attempt to counter Gordo's punch with one of your own, and your fists meet in midair and . . . *POW!* Gordo, unsurprisingly, plows right through you, his massive bulk lifting you into the air until . . . *Splash!* You come crashing down into the mud and won't be getting up . . .

YOU'RE KNOCKED OUT.
CONTINUE: Y/N?
Y: Head to 187 ●●●●   N: Head to 224 ●●

●●●

You move backward, and the card passes over your head, slicing a strand of hair as it flies by. You've avoided that attack, but the puppet draws and throws another card. Choose another move!

Head back to 27 ●●

●●●●

You veer to the right, and Sheriff Farmer grunts.

"I said to keep 'er steady, Deputy! There ain't no way I can get a shot with this here Spud Gun if you're weaving all over the road!"

Keep the car steady, and choose another move.

Head back to 153 ●●●●

You've made the leap across the gap, your fancy dress shoes just barely finding purchase on the floor. You windmill your arms frantically, trying to keep your balance on the edge of the steps, but it's not working! Magician or no, gravity is still one of the laws of the universe, and you begin to fall backward . . .

. . . and your foot finds the stairway! You stumble a bit, surprised, and then look behind you: You see the curve of the stairs leading down to the first floor, whole and unburnt. Everything in the mansion is as it should be, untouched. Another one of Nefario's illusions! Or was it? You can't be sure and realize that now that you've reached the second floor, you must be vigilant in debunking what is real and unreal in this place.

Out of the corner of your eye you see a flash of movement, and you turn instantly, a throwing card at the ready, to face whatever challenge the game is about to present—only to realize that the challenge is YOURSELF. For on the second-floor landing, there are no doors. There's only the small landing, in the middle of which is a solitary mirror, and in the middle of the mirror, there's only your reflection, standing there with your card. But the image in the glass wobbles and wavers, changing from your reflection to reveal a large card placed on an easel, the type of thing one would use to announce a different act in a performance, and that's exactly what this is! It reads:

The image of the easel fades back into your reflection, and as it does, you hear Nefario speak again, from nowhere and everywhere at once. It's apparent from his skill at throwing his voice that he must have trained extensively as a ventriloquist. The fiend!

"So, magician—you've made it past my illusion and to the second act. I guess it's true what they say—the show must go on! Or will it? Can you make it through my hall of mirrors to save the next guest? Ha ha ha ha ha ha!"

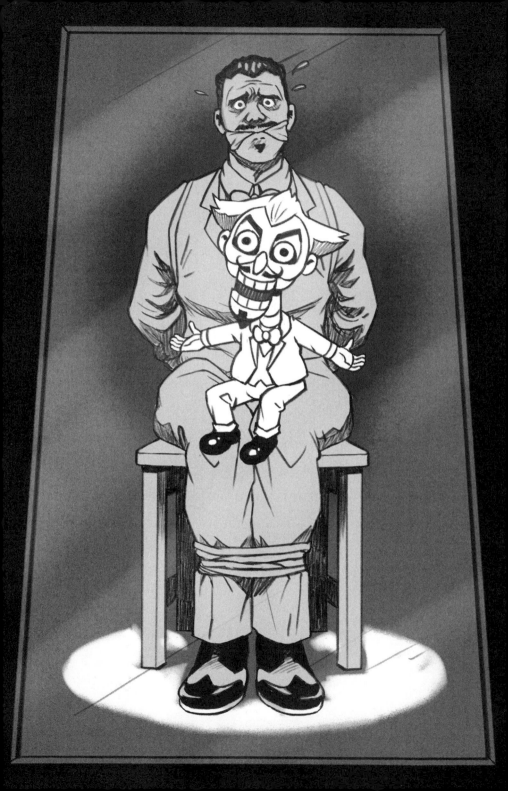

As he says this, the image in the mirror before you changes again, only this time you see Tommy, sitting in a chair, bound and gagged. On his lap, there sits . . . a smiling ventriloquist dummy, one that looks exactly like Nefario. Creepy!

"Come find me, magician," says the dummy. "If you dare!"

And then the image transforms again, turning back into your reflection, but only for a moment. As if on hinges, the mirror swings open like a door. Beyond, there is darkness. As there is nowhere else to go, you cross the threshold and step behind the mirror . . .

Head to 14 ●●●

●●

You dive to the left, and the bomb explodes in front of your car! You both shield your eyes from the debris coming your way, and the Goose Gang is gone. They've vamoosed! Or, rather, vamGOOSED.

"Dang it!" sighs Sheriff Farmer, "we almost had 'em."

THAT'S THE END, PEOPLE!
CONTINUE: Y/N?
Y: Head to 153 ●●●●   **N: Head to 224** ●●

●●●

You try to use your fan of cards to defend yourself from the vampire dummy, but instead it just sinks its wooden teeth into your leg, causing you to drop your cards. You hear the puppet Nefario laugh triumphantly as the other monstrous dummies leap from their perches and descend upon you. Unfortunately . . .

YOU ARE DEAD. CONTINUE: Y/N?
Y: Head to 131 ●●●●   **N: Head to 224** ●●

●●●●

You swing your rolling pin at Granny Goose, and she easily evades your wild blow. Choose another move.

Head back to 2 ●●●

●

Instead of going in for the final blow, you dance around Gordo, giving him the time to recover.

"You made one heck of a mistake, Deputy," he says, right before he winds up for a punch. *WHAM!* Gordo connects, right in the kisser! You zigged when you should have zagged, and now . . .

YOU'RE KNOCKED OUT.
CONTINUE: Y/N?
Y: Head to 199 ●●●●   **N: Head to 224 ●●**

●●

You disappear as Nefario's flaming card passes through where you were just standing. Quick thinking! But just as you reappear, Nefario throws ANOTHER flaming card. Move again!

Head back to 79 ●

●●●

You rush toward Granny Goose, which actually proves to be a good strategy because the strength of her swing causes her to whip around in a circle. But she's coming back at you with another swing, so act fast!

Head back to 156 ●●●●

●●●●

You move your body to the right, and Doc nods in approval. "That's good, kid. If someone's hammering you from the left, move to the right!"

Continue your training and head back to 57 ●●●● to try another move. If you've tried them all, head to 187 ●●●●

●

You deftly draw a card and, with a flick of your wrist, send it flying toward the leaping rabbit . . . and strike it directly in its center, shattering it into a thousand sharp pieces! You've destroyed one stained-glass rabbit, and the other two have stopped their pursuit, eyeing you warily.

Head to 201 ●●●

●●

You lean over to the left and move right into Granny's swing, which is so powerful that it knocks you into the air and off the train! You hang there for a moment, and then plummet toward the ground as Doc (still playing his banjo) and Granny watch you fall. Well, Deputy . . .

YOU'RE FINISHED! CONTINUE: Y/N?
Y: Head to 9 ●●●   N: Head to 224 ●●

●●●

You present your deck of cards in your signature shielding move, an act of dexterity that impresses Hercules not in the slightest, which you figure out when the rabbit overtakes you, scatters your cards, and leaps upon you with its impressive bulk. Your show is over, and . . .

YOU ARE DEAD. CONTINUE: Y/N?
Y: Head to 164 ●   **N:** Head to 224 ●●

●●●●

You honk the horn at the bouncing bomb, which predictably does absolutely nothing except make the bomb EXPLODE right in the jalopy's grille. Your chase is OVER!

THAT'S THE END, PEOPLE!
CONTINUE: Y/N?
Y: Head to 183 ●●   **N:** Head to 224 ●●

●

You try to move away from the open trapdoor, but you aren't quick enough, and instead you fall into its dark depths. Down, down, down, disappearing into nothingness . . .

GAME OVER. CONTINUE: Y/N?
Y: Head to 79 ●   **N:** Head to 224 ●●

●●

In a rash, foolhardy rush of magical bravado, you decide to move back DOWN the stairs, directly into the oncoming blaze. Well, we can chalk that decision up to the strange, twitchy responses that sometimes get the best of gamers, because as you jump into the fire, you learn quite quickly that this magical flame is very, very, VERY hot. Show's over, magician . . .

YOU ARE DEAD. CONTINUE: Y/N?
Y: Head to 214 ●   N: Head to 224 ●●

●●●

You honk the jalopy's horn at the bomb, which, predictably, does nothing to halt its explosion. *BOOM!* The blast sends the jalopy flipping through the air and through a nearby shopwindow. Your pursuit has ended!

THAT'S THE END, PEOPLE!
CONTINUE: Y/N?
Y: Head to 168 ●●   N: Head to 224 ●●

●●●●

You back up, unsure of where Nefario has disappeared to . . . and back directly into Nefario, who's appeared behind you! You spin around just in time to see him draw a card from his deck and slash sideways, down, and up with it. It's razor sharp, this card, and Nefario wields it like the weapon it is. Sadly, it's . . .

GAME OVER. CONTINUE: Y/N?
Y: Head to 79 ●   N: Head to 224 ●●

●

You picked . . .

. . . the Devil Card!
The beautifully illustrated playing card feels important and precious, like it holds some sort of strange secret. Professional curiosity takes hold of you, and being an avid collector of magical memorabilia (even if you're just playing a magician

in a video game, you're still a magician), you carefully place the card in the pocket on the inside of your jacket. Then, you turn and walk through the gap where the mirror was—it has silently disappeared while you were dealing with the devil in the crystal ball.

Head to 14 ●●●

●●

You pick up the piece of paper with the words "HTAED TNATSNI," and as you do, you hear Nefario's laughter. "You should learn to read more carefully, magician. It might just save your life!" You hear a terrific cracking noise as the floor beneath you falls apart, revealing . . . nothing! Everything in the room falls into the void.

YOU ARE DEAD. CONTINUE: Y/N?
Y: Head to 14 ●●●   N: Head to 224 ●●

●●●●

Instead of going toward the floating ball of swamp light, you walk back along the path you just came down, directly into the waiting grasp of the sentient swamp vines . . .

YOU ARE DEAD. CONTINUE: Y/N?
Y: Head to 172 ●   N: Head to 224 ●●

You didn't get any Devil Cards? Not a single one? Ah, that's too bad. You missed out on a really special treat. Finding nothing in your jacket pocket, you turn to your audience, hold your arms open wide, and take a bow. They clap with appreciation—you did save them from the mad magician, after all—and they rise to their feet. As they applaud, you sneakily use your magician's skills to cause a puff of smoke to erupt at your feet, obscuring you in a cloud of vanishing smoke, which fills your vision until you can see nothing else. The theater has disappeared, the applause becoming fainter and fainter as another sound replaces it: the sound of arcade games! As the smoke clears, you can see that you're no longer inside *Magician's Gambit*—you've returned to your own world!

If you want to play *Wild Goose Chase!*, head to 205 ●●

If you've completed both games, head to 224 ●●

●●

You move to the right of the aisle and try to climb onto some luggage, but Granny Goose's rolling pin is too wide and quick for you. It knocks you and Doc for a loop, stunning you for long enough that by the time you two recover, she's made her escape. Alas, Deputy . . .

YOU'RE FINISHED! CONTINUE: Y/N?
Y: Head to 93 ●●●   N: Head to 224 ●●

●●●

You counter Nefario's throw with one of your own, and your cards meet in midair. Their impact causes both of them to EXPLODE . . . showering the stage and the front rows of the theater in flower petals. Wow, this magic stuff sure is strange. But you've deflected Nefario's attack. Well done!

Head to 127 ●●

●●●●

You leap up into the air . . . directly into the path of Granny Goose's rolling pin! *WHACK!* The next thing you know, you're seeing stars, little flying birdies, and odd punctuation bits floating around your head . . . and Doc's face.

"Sorry, Deputy," Doc says sadly as he plays his banjo. "You've been out for a while, and Granny . . . well, she got away."

You sit up, dejected. You almost had her. Almost! But now . . .

YOU'RE FINISHED! CONTINUE: Y/N?
Y: Head to 93 ●●●   **N:** Head to 224 ●●

●

You rush forward to where Nefario disappeared from, hoping to grab the tails of his tux, but as you move, you hear the sound of the magician's friend—and enemy, it seems—the release of a hidden trapdoor! Instead of tackling Nefario, you fall into a dark hole in the stage, tumbling into nothingness.

GAME OVER. CONTINUE: Y/N?
Y: Head to 79 ●   **N:** Head to 224 ●●

●●

Sensing that the geese are going to migrate to the left fork, you turn the wheel that way . . .

. . . and you're right! You're right behind the geese, and you and your posse are still in this chase.

Head to 155 ●●

●●●

You move closer to the water tank, but it's not going anywhere. Inside, Amelia shrugs at you, as if to say, *What are you DOING?* Try something more dynamic, something more show business.

Head back to 154 ●

●●●●

You drop a handful of vanishing powder and turn into a phantom momentarily, only to reappear a second later in the same spot you were standing in. But Hercules has gotten wise to your tricks, and he is now standing inches away from you, drum raised over his head, which he brings down on YOUR head with a crash! Sadly . . .

YOU ARE DEAD. CONTINUE: Y/N?
Y: Head to 184 ●●● **N: Head to 224** ●●

●

BRONK! BRONK! You hit the jalopy's horn, making both Sheriff Farmer and Doc jump.

"I think you should stick to driving here, kid," says Doc. You heard the banjo-playing dog: Choose another move.

Head back to 216 ●●

●●

You disappear just as the werewolf and vampire dummies would have sunken their teeth into you, reappearing as they hit the wall behind you. The other dummies hiss and look at you as the werewolf and vampire turn and leap toward you again. Choose another move!

Head back to 17 ●

●●●

You move away from the water tank . . . directly into the path of Hercules, who wastes no time in knocking you to the ground and hopping on your prone body, making you disappear in a very . . . innovative manner.

YOU ARE DEAD. CONTINUE: Y/N?
Y: Head to 154 ●   N: Head to 224 ●●

●●●●

Instead of going in for the kill, for some reason you jump back for the chill. What?! This gives Gordo a crucial second to clear his head and shake off his dizziness, and as he does, a crafty smile plays out over his beak.

"You should have taken your shot when you had a chance, Deputy. Now it's my turn!"

Gulp.

Head back to 187 ●●●●

●

You block Li'l Nefario's card, but it reaches into its miniature pack for another weapon. Move again!

Head back to 27 ●●

●●

Surprised by your quick response, Nefario reels for a moment and then unleashes a volley of disappearing powder, vanishing from the stage in a cloud of multicolored smoke. Where has he gone? What do you do?

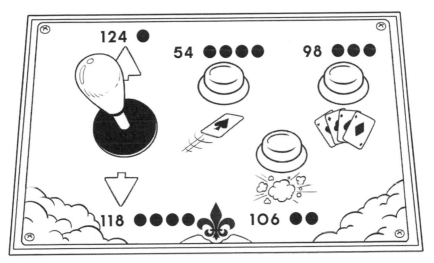

●●●

The train has come to a stop, and you, Sheriff Farmer, and Doc (playing wild runs on his banjo) disembark, Granny Goose in custody. The moment you step off the train, flashbulbs pop and sizzle—someone's alerted the press! You and your friends shield your eyes from the glare, while the old bird snarls at the assembled crowd of onlooking animated animals and the reporters all angling to get a story. If you didn't know Granny Goose was a waterfowl, you would swear, based purely on the sounds she was making, that she was actually some sort of hideous combination of wolf and snake.

"Granny Goose," shouts one reporter, an intrepid creature that kind of looks like a mutt with a mustache. "How does it feel to finally have your crime career crushed in mid-escape?"

"It was a frame-up!" Granny yells, still snarling. "These coppers hung an armed robbery racket on a poor ol' goose just trying to make an honest livin'."

"An honest living?" Sheriff Farmer says in disbelief. "Why, Granny, you and your Wild Goose Gang were public enemies number one, two, and three in Farmingtonville, from the Great Milk Shake-Up to the Hay Bale Connection to this latest escapade. You oughta be PROUD of such an illustrious career of criminal shenanigans and take credit for it!" The assembled crowd laughs at the sheriff's jest as Granny gets hopping mad and starts exclaiming curses that have no place in a nice video game like this. Nodding to the sheriff, representatives of the local constabulary take custody of Granny and escort her to the back of their gloriously goofy-looking wagon and shut the door behind her. As they drive off, alarm ringing, Granny Goose looks out through the bars in the back door and continues her off-color, unprintable rant.

"!#$@*!" Granny yells at the assembled crowd, forcing a mother hen in attendance with a string of chicks to put a hand over one chick's ear on one end and another chick's ear on the other and push all of their heads together to prevent them from hearing any more. But moments later, Granny Goose's curses have faded, and the hen releases her grip. Immediately one of the chicks asks, "Mama, what does '!#$@*!' mean?" causing the crowd to laugh uproariously. It's always funny when a baby chicken says "!#$@*!"—trust us.

"Say, Sheriff Farmer," says another reporter, a slick-looking cat. "Sparky Cat here from the *Farmingtonville Flyer*. Care to give us a quote about how you single-handedly brought the entire Wild Goose Gang to justice?"

"Well, I . . . ," Sheriff Farmer begins, and then pauses. He looks at you. "I couldn't have done it without the driving, boxing, and train-riding skills of my new deputy. If you want to get the real story, this is the person you want to talk to. I believe they have a great future in the field of cartoon-farm law enforcement."

Sheriff Farmer pushes on your back gently, making you step forward into a buzz of questions and flurry of flashes. As you try to make heads or tails of the activity around you, you can hear Doc rip into the game's theme music, and you realize you've done it—you've beaten *Wild Goose Chase!* And because you have, you feel it's time for you to leave this wacky and weird world. Your body starts to break into digital bits, and you know that it's time to make another choice.

If you want to play *Magician's Gambit*, head to 89 ●●

If you've beaten both games, head to 224 ●●

●●●●

The werewolf ventriloquist dummy lies on the floor of the weird room, and all the other monstrous dummies on the wall have now come to life and are watching the contest, their bizarre eyes ablaze with evil interest.

"Well . . . ," shouts the miniature Nefario impatiently to the vampire dummy. "Slay this magician!"

At Nefario's command, the wooden *nosferatu* scuttles forward on the ground toward you, like some sort of undead ventriloquist bug! What's your move?

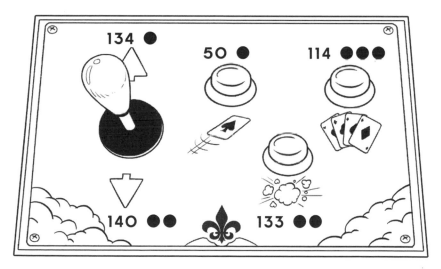

●

That's not going to work here. You might get a chance to fight later, though. Keep at it and choose another action.

Head back to 41 ●

●●

Poof! You disappear just as the scary stained-glass rabbit is about to sink its teeth into you, reappearing a few feet ahead, just in time for it to leap at you again! Choose another move.

Head back to 100 ●●●

●●●

You rush directly toward Granny Goose, and it's lucky for you that her rolling pin throw went off to the right, because otherwise you'd have been clobbered! The pin returns to her hand, and she makes haste out of the car, you and Doc following!

Head to 9 ●●●

● ● ● ●

You raise your cards to protect you against Hercules's charge, but as the giant magical rabbit collides with you and sends you flying through the air, you realize that that sort of defense might be better against projectiles, blinding lights, and other things of that ilk. Well, it DOES take a lot of practice to learn magic, but now . . .

YOU ARE DEAD. CONTINUE: Y/N?
Y: Head to 154 ●   N: Head to 224 ●●

●

That move won't work here. Try a different one.
Head back to 144 ●●

●●

POOF! You vanish in a cloud of smoke and reappear on the other side of the room . . . just as the vampire ventriloquist dummy leaps from the floor and fastens its wooden teeth in your neck, teeth that are quite sharp for a dummy. You try to shake it off, but the dummy holds tight, and . . .

YOU ARE DEAD. CONTINUE: Y/N?
Y: Head to 131 ●●●●   N: Head to 224 ●●

The floor slips away from you, and although you try to grab the edge of the stage, you can't get a grip, and you drop down through the trapdoor. You expect to land on a soft cushion of some sort, but nothing happens. You just fall and fall and fall.

GAME OVER. CONTINUE: Y/N?

Y: Head to 79 ● **N:** Head to 224 ●●

●●●●

You wind up your right fist, windmilling your arm a couple of times, and then—*WHAM!*—you pop Gordo right in the kisser with your LEFT hand, stunning him for a moment! Gordo looks at you with anger and not a little bit of surprise.

"Okay, that was the only one you're gonna get, punk. Let's dance!" He puts up his goose dukes.

Head to 162 ●●

●

You walk forward and KICK the crawling vampire dummy, sending it flying into the wall. Its body shatters into pieces, each of which continues to move, however ineffectually. Good work!

Head to 27 ●●

You approach the right mirror and see your reflection getting closer as you do. You reach out to touch its surface . . . and your hand passes through as easily as it would if the glass were made out of water!

You reach in, and your hand disappears into your reflection until your entire arm is plunged into the mirror. Weird, but interesting. So interesting that you decide to see how much farther you can go: You place a foot in the mirror, and then your entire body, holding your breath and closing your eyes as you do.

Opening your eyes, you see that you're . . . back in the room you were just in, only everything is now somehow different. Slightly off. But you can't put your finger on it. There is one major difference that is immediately apparent, though: Whereas before there was a crystal ball on the table, now there are three slips of paper. Moving closer, you see each one has something written on it, but you can't make out exactly what the words on the papers are.

As seemingly random as everything else you have encountered so far, you realize that what you thought were words were really just collections of letters.

They look like this:

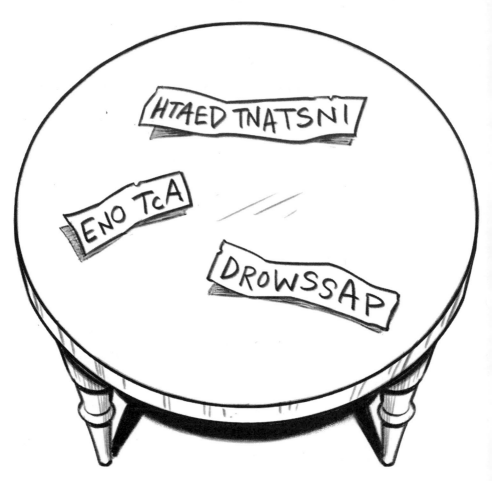

You feel an urge to take one of the strange pieces of paper, but which one?

If you take the paper with HTAED TNATSNI on it, head to 120 ●●

If you take the paper with ENO TCA on it, head to 103 ●●●

If you take the paper with DROWSSAP on it, head to 83 ●●●

● ● ●

Just as Sheriff Farmer's about to fire his Spud Gun, you accelerate the jalopy, sending it flying down the road . . . and passing the Goose Gang!

"Whoa, whoa, whoa, whoa!" yells Sheriff Farmer, barely holding on to the side of the jalopy. "We ain't in no auto-mo-bile race here, kid! We're in a dangerous car chase. There's a difference! And we're losing 'em!"

Sure enough, you've passed the geese, and when you turn to see how far ahead you've gotten, they've disappeared! You slow the jalopy and stop, and Doc (still playing his banjo) comments laconically from the back seat, "Why, I do believe that's the first time I've ever seen a police chase end by the police beating the crooks in a race. Huh."

THAT'S THE END, PEOPLE!
CONTINUE: Y/N?
Y: Head to 155 ● ●   N: Head to 224 ● ●

• • • •

"No! Noooooooooo!" screams Nefario as he pounds futilely on the lid of the coffin from the inside. "There's gotta be a latch in here somewhere . . ."

But it's too late. The enchanted saw bites into the wood of the coffin like a magic knife through magic butter, sending sawdust flying as it rapidly moves back and forth. The saw cuts all the way through the coffin, slicing it in half and separating Nefario into two sections! His torso and legs tumble in separate directions, but astoundingly, there's no blood! Instead, a thick, dark mist oozes out of each part of his bifurcated body. The legs push the lower half toward the backstage area, while Nefario's upper half furiously pulls itself along the floor, chasing after them. He has time, however, to spit insults at you.

"You may have won THIS magical battle, but the show must go on! Just you wait until you see what I have in store for my next show. Why, this is NOTHING compared to thaaaaaa—"

Nefario's rant is cut short, though, for the inky smoke leaking out of him has intensified, consuming what's left of his body and leaving nothing but scorch marks on the stage. Gross.

"Well, say what you will about Nefario," says Professor Carter as he dismounts the stage, "he certainly does know how to wrap up a show." When he gets to his family, they quickly check to make sure that he's okay before they all take their seats and look at you expectantly. "But the question is," Professor Carter continues, "do YOU?"

You have successfully defeated Nefario and freed his captives, who have gathered before you in the theater's seats. Are they expecting an encore?

"Come on now, magician," says Tommy. "The show can't end like that. What's your grand finale?"

"Indeed," says Amelia.

Amazing. It appears that they haven't gotten their fill of magic, despite the weird events of the night. You look around, thinking. Your magical gas tank is running on empty; you've exhausted your bag of tricks over the course of the evening in your quest to triumph over Nefario and free his prisoners, and now they want more? Ah, audiences. Your mind races as you struggle to come up with a real showstopper, and . . .

Wait. Look in the inside pocket of your coat: Did you happen to find any of the Devil Cards hidden throughout the mansion? If so, how many did you get?

If you found one Devil Card, turn to 104 ●●●●
If you found two Devil Cards, turn to 216 ●●●
If you found three Devil Cards, turn to 197 ●●●
If you didn't find any Devil Cards, turn to 121 ●

●

You rush toward Granny Goose again, and this time she's ready for you, moving to the side at the last second and then pushing you as you pass, knocking you off the train completely. That . . . was not good deputy work, and now . . .

YOU'RE FINISHED! CONTINUE: Y/N?
Y: Head to 9 ●●●   **N: Head to 224** ●●

●●

You back away from the creepy crawler and stay just out of its reach, its carved wooden claws grasping for you but not able to get a hold on you. You can't keep this up forever, though. Choose another move!

Head back to 131 ●●●●

● ● ●

You stumble backward, knocking the coffin out of the saw's path, but find yourself now directly in its crosshairs . . . if a saw had crosshairs. Now it's . . .

GAME OVER. CONTINUE: Y/N?
Y: Head to 79 ●   N: Head to 224 ●●

● ● ● ●

You and Doc try to flatten yourselves against the side of the aisle, but there's no room—Granny Goose's rolling pin collides with you both, knocking you down and giving her time to escape! Wrong move, Deputy . . .

YOU'RE FINISHED! CONTINUE: Y/N?
Y: Head to 93 ●●●   N: Head to 224 ●●

●

Instead of doing anything proactive, you decide to walk away from the water tank . . . directly into the arms of Hercules, who wraps its paws around you and begins to squeeze. You struggle to free yourself, but this is one death-defying experience that you cannot actually defy.

YOU ARE DEAD. CONTINUE: Y/N?
Y: Head to 184 ●●●   N: Head to 224 ●●

●●

You spread your cards in a protective shield, and it holds them off for only a second. Make another choice!

Head back to 17 ●

●●●

Deciding to press your luck, you rapidly advance toward Granny Goose . . . and she runs backward, not expecting your rush! Good move, Deputy!

Head to 66 ●●●

●●●●

In one smooth motion, you take the cards from your pocket and fan the entire deck in front of you, forming a barrier between you and whatever you're facing. Something tells you that this would be an effective defense against attacks on your person. Good to know.

Head back to 89 ●● to try another move, and if you've tried them all, head to 192 ●

The saw is descending, getting even closer to the coffin, and the downed Nefario makes a gesture. "It's time YOU vanished, magician!" he yells. You hear the unmistakable clicking of a trapdoor being deployed and sense the ground starting to give way—the trapdoor is underneath you!

What's your next move?

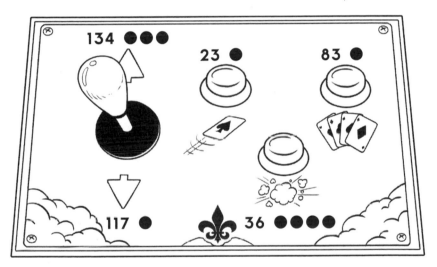

Or have you?

The geese's car has come to a stop, its tires flat, its engine whistling, and its radiator steaming. Inside the car, there seems to be a bit of a kerfuffle going on. You, Sheriff Farmer, and Doc (still playing his banjo) get out of the jalopy and cautiously approach the vehicle, when suddenly the doors are flung open, and out jump three geese.

"Granny Goose, Goober Goose, and Gordo Goose!" says Sheriff Farmer. "You stop right there and come with me and my deputy here. Your crime wave is over!"

"You think so, Sheriff Farmer?" says the goose in the middle, a sly, oily-looking specimen.

"I know so, Goober!" retorts Sheriff Farmer as he advances toward the geese, Spud Gun in hand. But as he walks forward, Goober pulls something from behind his back: another bomb, which he lobs toward Sheriff Farmer!

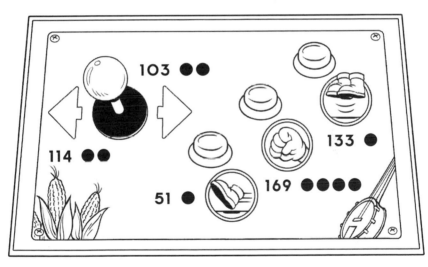

You approach the stained-glass window and realize it's a portrait of your archenemy, Nefario! But how did he manage to install such an elaborate piece of artwork without anybody knowing it?

"You certainly would like to know, wouldn't you?" says the glass image of Nefario. "It will just have to remain my secret, I suppose. It's one of the MANY reasons that I'm a better magician than you will ever be. As is this."

The stained-glass Nefario reaches into the glass top hat he's holding and pulls out a rabbit, then another, and then yet another, until he holds three of them in his hand, dangling them by their long, floppy ears. Then, he

tosses them toward you, and somehow the rabbits break free of the window and land on the floor in front of you! They've grown in the transition and are now the size of large dogs, but they're still made of glass and lead, their flat bodies moving oddly. Their cute buckteeth have extended into fangs made of sharp shards of glass. They begin to slowly hop toward you.

"Ta-daa!" says the stained-glass Nefario, spreading his hands and winking at you, his face freezing into a grin as whatever magic or illusion animating the window ceases. But although the window is now static, the rabbits are not . . . and they're still hopping toward you. Behind you is the hallway, ahead of you are the killer glass rabbits. What's your deal?

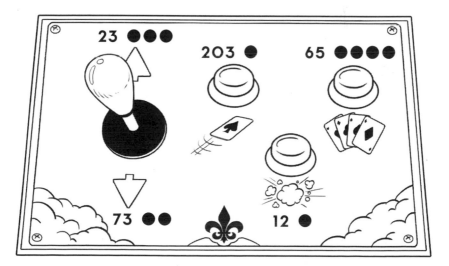

●●●●

You throw a card from your deck down the hall, but it finds no target to embed itself in, so it flits harmlessly away. Save the lethal magic tricks for when you're in a lethal magic fix. Choose another move.

Head back to 200 ●

●

You figure that there's no time like the present to go on the attack, so you rush toward Gordo with a flurry of punches. You've taken the enormous goose by surprise, and you land a body blow, a right cross, and a left hook in quick succession! The crowd goes silent, and Doc, the rooster referee, and Gordo look at you in wonder.

Head to 150 ●●●●

●●

You throw your vanishing powder, but instead of aiming it at yourself, you move your arm in a sweeping motion, first dousing Nefario with the magical dust and then covering Professor Carter in it. Both Nefario and Professor Carter disappear and reappear, only now, Professor Carter stands before you, and Nefario is in the coffin!

Head to 138 ●●●●

Pick a card—only one—and follow its instructions!

Head to 170 ●   **Head to 71** ●●   **Head to 102** ●

● ● ● ●

He's temporarily cross-eyed. What's your move?

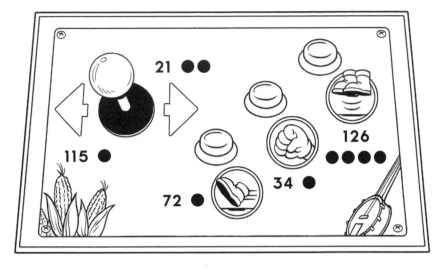

●

You attempt to slide forward off the coffin, but the saw slides into YOU. Sadly, it's . . .

GAME OVER. CONTINUE: Y/N?

Y: Head to 79 ●   **N: Head to 224** ● ●

● ●

Hands on the wheel, you turn it to the right. As expected, the wheels of the jalopy turn to the right.

Have you tried every control?

If not, head back to 205 ● ●

If you have, head to 219 ● ● ● ●

The impact against the tank has broken the glass's
fragile surface, and the pressure of the water against
that weak surface causes the tank to explode, sending
a torrent of water to flood the room! A wave crashes
against you and Hercules, but you manage to grab on to
Amelia's bound hands, and you both watch as the water
carries the magic rabbit away from the foyer, thrashing
and fighting against the aquatic onslaught all the way.

Soon, the flow of water slows and finally stops, leaving you and Amelia amid the wreckage of Nefario's water-tank trap. You stand and help her to her feet, untying her, and as you do, you hear Nefario's voice once again. Looking toward the stairs, you see that the menacing magician is standing on the landing, mere steps above you.

"So, you managed to effect an escape from my first little trap and save one of my captives, eh? Well, no matter—you still have two acts to go, my friend, and they are tough acts to follow . . . and survive!"

You leave Amelia behind as she rests and rush up the stairs toward Nefario, but before you can reach him he disappears in a cloud of smoke. Nothing is left but the echoes of his laughter and the smell of brimstone. *The show must go on*, you think, and you shuffle your cards as you go the only way you can: up the stairs, to the mansion's second floor!

Head to 214 ●

Phew! That was a close one! You managed to get the old lady sheep out of the way, and now you're even closer to the Goose Gang.

"Almost got 'em," Sheriff Farmer says. "Allllll-most. Keep it steady, Deputy! I think I've got a shot . . ."

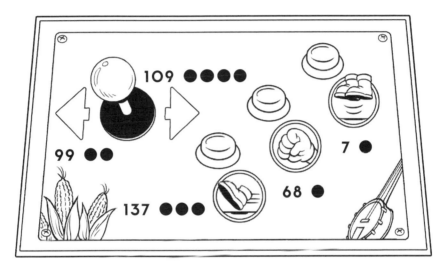

Time is running out! The glass of the water tank has been cracked by your card throw, but it still hasn't broken, and Amelia's still trapped inside. But Hercules the gigantic magic rabbit is now charging toward you. How will you get out of this fix?

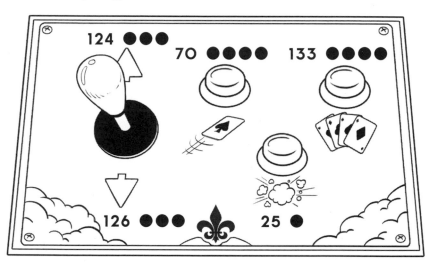

●●

You whiz around the corner, still in hot pursuit! Farmingtonville citizens run to and fro as the geese's car and the jalopy zoom down the avenue, all of them managing to avoid getting clobbered by the careening vehicles. All of them except for one: A little old lady sheep, seemingly oblivious to all the hubbub surrounding her, is walking calmly across the street! The geese weave around her just in the nick of time, but she's dead in your sights. You'd better move!

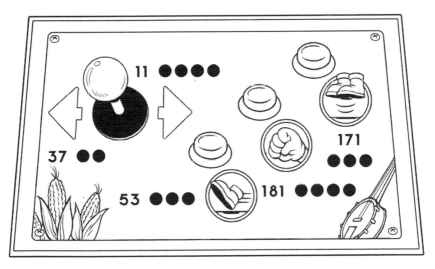

● ● ●

You hold up your shield of cards in front of your body, but the stained-glass rabbit dives for your legs and grabs hold. Its friends, seeing that it has you at a disadvantage, join in on attacking your lower extremities, and though you try to use your cards to destroy them, the cards tumble out of your hands in the confusion, and . . .

YOU ARE DEAD. CONTINUE: Y/N?
Y: Head to 100 ● ● ●   N: Head to 224 ● ●

● ● ● ●

You and Doc pop your heads out of the open train windows, the wind whipping your faces. The train's going along at a good clip now, and rocking back and forth.

"Where do you think she went, Deputy?" asks Doc, his banjo slung over his back, his words almost lost to the wind. You shrug in response, but then something catches your eye. Looking up, you see a figure racing along the top of the train, leaving a trail of flying money behind her. It's Granny—she's climbed on TOP of the locomotive and is rushing to the front of the train! You and Doc climb out the window and pull

yourselves up as well. Doc unslings his banjo, and as you two follow Granny Goose, he begins to play ominous creepy music.

Soon, you've closed the gap between you and Granny Goose, the trail of wind-whipped money still flying from her bag of loot, until you're just a few steps behind her. It looks as if you might actually nab this crook without any complications! But just as you're about to grab Granny, the train hits a corner and jolts, causing you, Doc, and Granny to all grab hold of something lest you be knocked off. The sudden motion also makes Doc hit a bum chord on his banjo, which causes Granny to turn around! Seeing you, her beady goose eyes narrow, and she raises her rolling pin . . . and drops it as the train jolts again! The pin rolls toward you, and you pick it up—you've got a weapon now! Granny Goose looks at you . . . and smiles a goosey grin.

"You think you've got me at a disadvantage, do ya?" she says. "Well, there's one thing you should know about old Granny Goose . . . ," she continues as she reaches into her bag of loot . . . and takes out another rolling pin! "I always have a backup plan. If you want to bring me in, you're gonna have to duel me!"

You're facing off against a mean old-lady goose armed

with a deadly rolling pin, both of you in a sword-fighting stance, when suddenly she swipes at you with her weapon! What's your move?

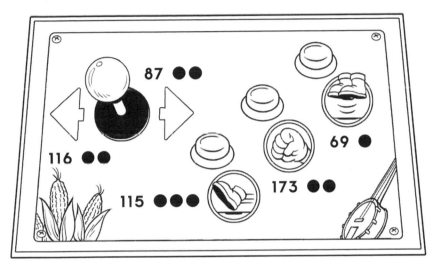

You draw from your deck and throw a card. It cuts through some flame, snuffing it out, and embeds itself in the door, but you'd have to throw a hundred decks to put out this fire or knock down that door. Choose another trick!

Head back to 192 ●

●●

Nice jump, Deputy. How about chasing after that larcenous goose you're after, though? Pick another move.

Head back to 41 ●

●●●

You rush toward Nefario's thrown card, and it strikes you square in the chest, its magical flame quickly setting your suit ablaze. The fire spreads rapidly, and before you know it, you are covered from head to toe in a magical conflagration. As you're consumed, you watch the saw cut through the coffin. What a depressing ending to the show. Not only was Nefario's trick literally a killer, it's now . . .

GAME OVER. CONTINUE: Y/N?
Y: Head to 79 ●   **N: Head to 224** ●●

●●●●

You poke your head out of the left window of the train and—*BONK!*—you take a rolling pin right to the head— Granny Goose was hanging in wait off the edge of the train, and you unluckily fell into her trap. Alas! Your last thought as you lose consciousness (accompanied by the sound of Granny's greasy laughter and Doc's mournful banjo picking) is . . .

YOU'RE FINISHED! CONTINUE: Y/N?
Y: Head to 9 ●●●   N: Head to 224 ●●

●

You flee from the encroaching vines and plunge into the darkness, but you get only a few feet before you realize that your legs are getting wet—you've wandered off the path through the swamp and into the swamp itself! You try to go back, but the mud holds you fast . . . and begins to pull you down, down, down. You grasp for anything, trying to get a hold to pull you up, but vines burst from the surface of the water and wrap around you, helping to finish the mud's job. You are pulled beneath the surface in seconds, and . . .

YOU ARE DEAD. CONTINUE: Y/N?
Y: Head to 35 ●●●   N: Head to 224 ●●

Impressed by your last punch, Gordo Goose has raised his fists in a defensive position, and he's dancing back and forth, trying to confuse you. Suddenly he lets loose with a solid right aimed directly at you. What's your move?

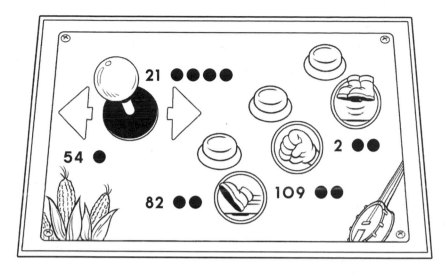

You walk toward the trio and spread your arms apart, displaying your empty hands. They stare at you raptly. Then you walk back to your original position. Impressive move.

Head back to 89 ●● to try another move, and if you've tried them all, head to 192 ●

●●●●

You juke to the left, practicing your dodges. Gordo Goose begins to look impatient. "C'mon, kid! I ain't got all day. I've got some candy to steal from some little piggies after this. Hit me!"

You'd better hurry up and start fighting before Gordo gets mad. Choose another move!

Head back to 187 ●●●●

You've finally made it to the mansion's foyer, and looking back at the hallway you just emerged from, you see that the distance from the library door to where you now stand is scarcely more than a few strides. You've broken free of Nefario's illusion and come to the end of the previously endless corridor. Presto!

You turn to the staircase that leads to the second floor, but your way is blocked by a large, four-sided glass tank, filled almost to the top with water. Hanging above the tank, bound hand and foot, is Amelia, her mouth gagged and her eyes wide with fright. Upon spotting you, she begins to thrash about.

"So, you've managed to stuff my rabbits back into the metaphorical hat, eh?" says Nefario's voice, but the dastardly deceiver is nowhere to be seen. You look around the foyer, but his voice is seemingly coming from all directions at once. Another trick! "Well, let's see if you have the magical moxie to effect THIS escape. Ha ha ha ha! Allow me to introduce you to the first of my assistants. Drumroll, please, Hercules."

You begin to move toward the water tank but pause when out of a dark corner of the room hops another rabbit. But instead of stained glass, this one seems to be real flesh and blood, or as real as a mangy six-foot-tall bunny standing on its hind legs, wearing a dirty vest and a tattered top hat, can be. Around its neck it wears a strap attached to a bass drum, upon which the bunny plays a menacing beat—*dum . . . dum . . . dum*—as it stares at you with its demented red eyes.

The bunny keeps staring.

Dum . . . dum . . . dum.

And staring.

Dum . . . dum . . . dum.

And staring some more.

This rabbit might be evil, but it is a very good drummer. And then, suddenly, it stops the drumroll. But it keeps staring at you.

CRACK! An unseen catch is released, and Amelia's suspension . . . is suspended! She falls straight down into the tank, whose lid immediately flips over and locks, seemingly pushed by an unseen hand. Amelia thrashes about in the water, panicking. Nefario's hollow, spooky laughter echoes through the hall.

"Hercules," shouts Nefario's disembodied voice, "make this impertinent prestidigitator DISAPPEAR!"

Hercules the rabbit screams an awful rabbit cry and begins advancing on you. Behind the creature, Amelia pounds on the tank's lid, but it won't budge. She looks at you, terrified, her eyes imploring you to free her. You know that you have only seconds to get to the tank and get her out, but your way is now blocked by a fierce anthropomorphic rabbit, which again plays a slow beat—*bam! . . . bam! . . . bam!*—on its drum as it advances toward you with DEATH in its eyes.

Hercules, the giant magical homicidal rabbit, is creeping toward you, beating its drum and keeping you from freeing Amelia, who's trapped in Nefario's water-tank death trap. Suddenly Hercules charges.

What's your play?

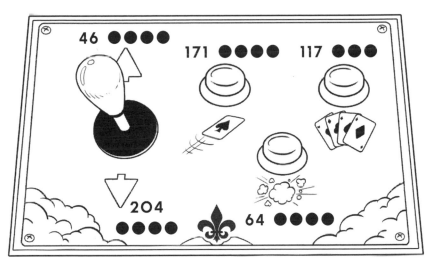

You're gaining on the carload of crooked geese. Suddenly one of the geese leans out of a window on the left side of the car and drops a bomb onto the road. What do you do?

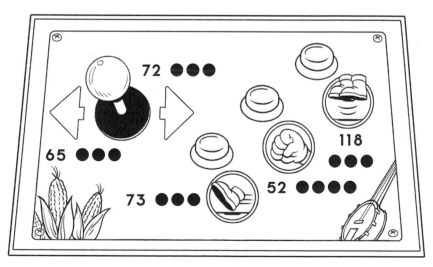

●●●

The vines shoot out toward you with astonishing swiftness, but your magically trained reflexes have made you accustomed to reacting to sudden changes, and you drop some vanishing powder, disappearing and then reappearing a little farther down the path, just out of the vines' reach. This works for now but won't work forever. Move again.

Head back to 172 ●

●●●●

You signal Sheriff Farmer, who catches your drift just as Goober Goose throws his bomb. A crack shot, Sheriff Farmer lets a spud fly and—*BOOM!*—it destroys Goober's missile in midair, forcing the greasy goose to quake and quiver on the ground. Seeing their bomb-throwing accomplice defeated, the other two geese speedily take off in different directions!

Head to 57 ●●●●

You got . . .

. . . the Death Card! Which means . . .

YOU ARE DEAD. CONTINUE: Y/N?

Y: Head to 222 ●   **N:** Head to 224 ●●

●●

You walk toward the tank, coming up to its cool surface. Just behind the glass, Amelia stares at you, wild-eyed and frantic. Bubbles float from her mouth—she's almost done for! There are no locks to pick, no secret levers to throw—you need to do something else.

Head back to 184 ●●●

●●●

HONK! HONK! HONK! You lean on the horn, waking the little old lady from her daze and forcing her to leap into the air and grab on to a lamppost to get out of your way. Nice strategy, Deputy!

Head to 153 ●●●●

●●●●

You throw one of your cards directly at Hercules, and it embeds itself in its rabbity flesh, slowing the monster for a moment, but just a moment: Your card tricks seem to be only an annoyance to the beast, and it quickly recovers and continues toward you. Choose another move.

Head back to 164 ●

Knowing that if you go back, you'll run into the homicidal vines, you press on. The only way is forward, so you walk deeper into the weird swamp and away from the gate.

You walk for a while, following the path as it winds through the nighttime swamp, strange vegetation pressing toward you from all sides. Just ahead in the humid mist, you can barely make out a bouncing light, seemingly calling to you, encouraging you to follow. You move faster, hoping to catch up to the light, but it gets farther and farther away. Is this floating bit of swamp gas leading you somewhere you need to be, or is it calling you to your doom?

The decision might not be yours to make, though. The hairs stand up on your neck, making your magician sense vibrate—you're being followed! Turning, you see a new set of swamp vines crawling toward you, aiming for your ankles!

What's your play?

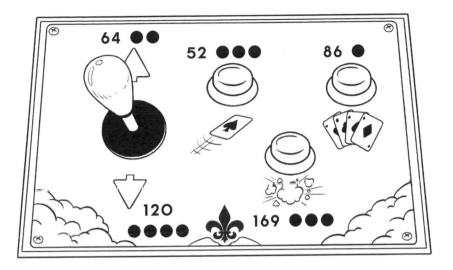

●●

You swing your rolling pin and meet Granny's in mid-swipe, the collision sending a shock down your arm. She growls at you again—boy, is this one mean goose. But you're in this fight. Good luck!

Head to 2 ●●●

●●●

You try to scoot back off the coffin, but the saw scoots down onto YOU. Sadly, it's . . .

GAME OVER. CONTINUE: Y/N?
Y: Head to 79 ●   N: Head to 224 ●●

••••

You, Doc (still playing his banjo), and Sheriff Farmer rush over to the train on the track to the right, just barely jumping through a still-open door on the side. Hoping you've made the right decision, you begin to stalk up the center corridor of the train, passing by a steady stream of animals that seem to be dressed a little bit . . . odd.

"Say, there's something mighty familiar about all these characters," says Sheriff Farmer, looking around.

"You got that right, Sheriff," says Doc as he starts to play a jaunty, rousing, almost . . . circus-like tune. "I just can't put my picking finger on it."

And that's when a motley group of rowdy animals dressed in outlandish and colorful clothes enter the car you're in, each of them jumping and flipping and tumbling over one another in what looks like organized chaos. Upon closer inspection, you can see that each one of the animals has its face and snout and such adorned in greasepaint—they're all clowns! Both Sheriff Farmer and Doc are correct: This is no ordinary train, it's . . .

"The circus train!" says the sheriff, taking off his hat and tossing it to the ground. "I should've known it. How did I miss that detail? Boy, some detective I turned out

to be. Well, it looks like the joke's on us, my friends. We chose the wrong train."

"But at least it's a downright entertaining one," says Doc as one of the clowns cartwheels past.

"Welp, we might as well explore the whole train, seeing as how we're stuck here and all," says the sheriff as he leads you farther into the train.

You and your friends walk through the rest of the circus train's cars, keeping an eye out for Granny Goose, but she's nowhere to be found—she's not hiding among the exotic animals, not with the trapeze cats or the acrobat dogs, not with the motorcycle monkeys, none of them. It seems that the old bird was too slick of a goose for you to catch. Finally, you, Doc, and the sheriff come to the circus train's chow car, where a bunch of performers are having their lunch. Walking up to the food line, you each grab a sandwich and a cup of hot chocolate and take a seat at a free table.

"I always wanted to run away and join the circus, but this ain't zactly what I had in mind," says Doc (still playing the banjo).

"It's too bad we lost Granny Goose," adds the sheriff. "I suppose I could flash my badge and have 'em stop the train, but I'm just too upset with m'self. If only there were some way we could have a do-over."

"Did someone say 'do-over'?" All three of you look up to see a new arrival at your table. A wolfish animal dressed in evening wear stands at the head, smiling under his thick mustache. "I think I might be able to help you with that. Do you mind if I sit with you?"

Without waiting for an answer, the wolf in snazzy clothes sits next to Doc, opposite you and the sheriff. "How do you folks do? I'm the circus's resident magician. I work in one of the tents in the sideshow, and I'm always looking for a chance to workshop a new trick. My latest one is a doozy—if it works, that is." The magician winks wolfishly. "First off, do any of you happen to have a pack of cards on you?"

You and the sheriff shake your heads, but Doc reaches into a pocket and takes out a deck. "Always got one on my person," he says, handing it to the magician. "Helps pass the time when I'm not a-banjoin'."

You and the sheriff nod, recognizing the wisdom of Doc's words. Who could be a-banjoin' all the time, anyway?

"Excellent!" cries the magician as he takes the cards out of the pack and begins to shuffle them at a blinding speed, finally stopping and dealing three cards before you, faceup. Instead of having the normal numbers, suits, or royalty on them, two of the cards depict a duck and one of them shows a goose.

"This trick is called Duck, Duck, Goose. I'm going to flip these cards over"—the magician does that—"and then mix them up, but please keep your eye on the Goose Card." You try to keep up, but his motions are too quick for you to follow. "You know where the Goose Card is, Deputy?" You shake your head no. "Excellent! Then that makes it even better. Y'see, if you pick out a Duck Card, you get nothing, but if you find the Goose Card, you get . . . well, you get a surprise. But you get only one try. Ready?"

You shrug, figuring that you might as well see what this strange magician is up to.

Head to 84 ●●　　**Head to 12** ●●　　**Head to 4** ●●●

With a fluid motion, you pull the pack of cards from your pocket, remove a card from the deck, and throw it directly toward your audience! It moves with uncanny speed . . . and slices into the whole watermelon sitting on the table in front of them, cutting it neatly in half. Your audience gasps in astonishment. That's one deadly deck you've got there! That would be an effective attack, should you ever need one.

Head back to 89 ●● to try another move, and if you've tried them all, head to 192 ●

Your disappearing act has landed you in an unusual place: directly on top of the coffin, as the saw gets ever closer!

"Ha ha ha ha!" Nefario does a little dance of joy and bows. "Thank you for giving me an idea for my NEXT big finale—sawing two people in half with one saw. Brilliant! But I'm afraid no one will know that it was your idea. Prepare to die, magician!"

The saw is inches away from your face—what's your play?

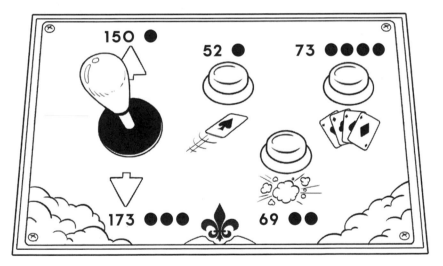

You unleash a rapid-fire series of missiles toward the flames, and each of your cards is turned to ash immediately. And what's worse, the inferno continues roaring up the steps. What did you think CARDS would do against a FIRE, anyway? Think again, magician!

Head back to 214 ●

●●●●

You elbow Sheriff Farmer, and he lets a spud fly in the old lady sheep's direction. The potato explodes at her feet, sending her hopping to the side of the road and out of your path. Keep on driving!

Head to 153 ●●●●

●

The head of the Nefario ventriloquist dummy is at your feet, its mouth still moving. You can hear the faint echo of words coming from its wooden throat, so you release Tommy from his bonds and kneel down to hear better (keeping your distance, of course—these sorts of things are known to bite).

"Well done, magician," says the dummy in Nefario's voice, wheezing a little. It coughs, and sawdust puffs out from between its lips. "But you've only seen act one and act two, and as everyone in our profession knows, it's act three that you have to watch out for. Ha ha ha ha ha ha!"

The glassy orbs in the ventriloquist dummy's head turn up until you can see only the whites of the eyes. Its wooden body lies in a heap on the floor, still twitching a little, and you can hear the echo of Nefario's laughter fading. You've survived the deadly second act of his show, but what could your sinister rival have up his sleeve for a finale?

In answer to your mental question, a panel on one of the walls moves aside under its own power, revealing a hidden set of stairs that wind upward. Knowing that there's nowhere to go but up, you wave goodbye to Tommy and enter the secret passageway, shuffling your cards in one hand, ready to face the final curtain.

Head to 55 ●●●

You've avoided the last bomb the geese have thrown and gained on their car, but it looks like they're preparing another explosive to send your way. You'd better stop them from throwing it before it's too late!

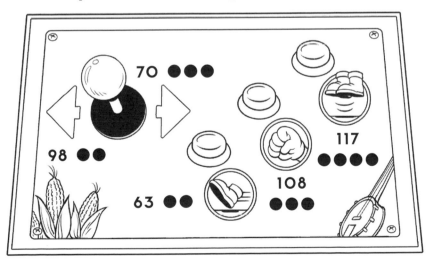

● ● ●

You stand between the tank of water and Hercules the rabbit, who is just beginning to notice that you're behind it! You're facing the tank, and you can see that Amelia is running out of air inside. What's your deal?

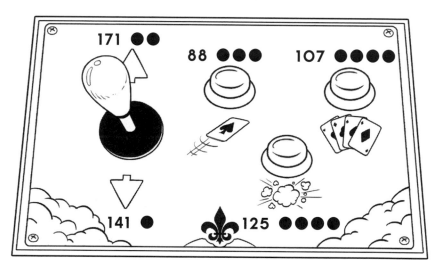

●●●●

You veer to the right side of the road, driving directly into the front of a store called the Chicken Co-op. Feathers fly as the car crashes into the structure, and Sheriff Farmer is thrown to the back of the shop. He rises from behind the counter.

"Looks like the Wild Goose Gang has gotten away," he says, spitting chicken feathers from his mouth. "Are you SURE you're my new deputy? You sure don't DRIVE like one."

THAT'S THE END, PEOPLE!
CONTINUE: Y/N?
Y: Head to 219 ●●●● **N: Head to 224** ●●

●

You selected . . .

. . . the Death Card! Which unfortunately means that . . .

YOU ARE DEAD.
CONTINUE: Y/N?
Y: Head to 14 ●●●
N: Head to 224 ●●

You open the door on the right cautiously, wary of whatever inside is making the fearsome growling noises. Cards at the ready, you enter . . .

. . . and find yourself in a small room, barren except for a table, on which there is an old-time record player, the kind with a large, bell-shaped horn for a speaker. An album is spinning on the record player, and as you creep closer, you realize that the growling sounds are coming from the speaker! You lift the needle off the record, stopping the growls, and hold the disc up for inspection. The label reads:

You can hear the disembodied laughter of Nefario echo in the room. It was a gag, and you've wasted time! Hoping that this delay doesn't mean something terrible has happened, you throw the record against the wall, shattering it into pieces, and rush out of the room and back to the hallway.

Head back to 201 ●●●

●●●

You walk up to the mirror on the left, and as you do, your reflection . . . shifts. It gets smaller, as if you were looking at the kind of mirror that distorts your reflection and makes you wider or, in this case, shorter. Strange. It's just like you are in some sort of carnival, which you are, in a way.

You reach out and touch the mirror's surface. It's solid. When you press harder, nothing happens. It doesn't budge. Or do a single magical thing.

But wait . . . do you have the DROWSSAP paper?

If you have the DROWSSAP paper,
go to 17 ●

If you don't have the DROWSSAP paper,
go to 14 ●●●

●●●●

Your lightning-fast training session over, Doc leads you out of the locker room, down a dark corridor toward a set of double doors. The banjo-playing dog turns to you.

"All right, kid," Doc says. "Boxing here in Farmingtonville is pretty much like boxing everywhere: You wanna hit yer opponent more times than they hit you and make 'em kiss the mud before you do. Got it?"

You nod. As if you had a choice.

"Well, okay then. Let's go."

Doc pushes open the doors, and light floods your eyes: You're in a giant outdoor arena, at the center of which is a rough boxing ring surrounded by . . . a pit of mud? Surrounding the ring are rows and rows of rowdy animals, all of them spoiling to see some action.

You follow Doc down an aisle that leads directly to one of the corners of the ring.

"Get on in that there ring and get to punchin'. I'll coach you from yer corner," Doc says (still playing the banjo).

You climb through the ropes of the ring. All around you, animals are hooting and hollering and cheering and generally going bonkers. At the side of the ring, a cow rings its cowbell to announce that the fight is about to get underway. A rooster dressed in a black-and-white referee jersey climbs into the ring. As it does, an old-timey microphone drops mysteriously from the sky. At the center of the ring, the rooster grabs the microphone and begins to speak, its announcer's voice booming through the Pig Pen.

"Good evening, all you good farm animals, and welcome to tonight's main event, what's sure to be a titanic tussle, a mighty match, a bee-yoo-tiful battle, a real wang-dang-doodle of a fight, yessiree! Are you excited? Come on, I said, 'Are you excited?' Lemme hear you!"

The animals go WILD! Hey—they live on a farm, but they're wild animals. WILD ANIMALS ON A FARM. Get it? Okay, anyway.

"In this corner we have our challenger, weighing an indeterminate number of pounds, the short arm of the law, the new-in-town, pint-size pugilist known only as the DEPUTY!"

You raise your arms, and the animals moo you, bah you, quack you, and boo you. Boo who? Boo YOU, that's who. Boo-hoo.

"And in that corner, we've got our current cham-peen, weighing a whole lotta pounds. It's the foulest fowl this side of Old MacDonald's Farm. You know him, you fear him, you don't wanna get near him, it's GORDO GOOOOOOOOOSE!"

The crowd goes hog wild this time! It's a real jamboree out there.

"Don't worry about it, kid," Doc says. "They're always like that when a challenger steps into th' ring. Just keep your hands up and punch him occasionally!"

And then, the cow at the edge of the ring strikes its cowbell again. It's time to fight!

You cautiously move to the center of the ring and meet Gordo Goose there. The enormous villain hasn't even raised his feathered fists in preparation to fight, he looks so confident.

"Tell you what, Deputy," he honks. "Howsabout I give you the first lick? You get a freebie. C'mon!"

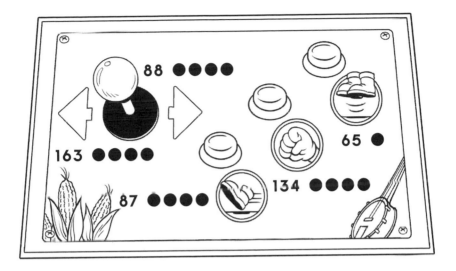

"What a show, what a show," says the older gentleman as he rises to shake your hand. "I am so pleased to have engaged you for this private event, here in my strange and beautiful mansion in the Garden District of New Orleans. I shall send the word out to the rest of the Society of Wealthy Eccentrics (of which I am the president) to further engage your services. And the word of Merlin Carter, amateur professor of parapsychology and chair of the society, goes far around here. What did you think, Tommy?"

"I must admit that I was skeptical, Uncle Merle," says the young man, loosening his tie. "I've seen some wild things both uptown and downtown, but nothing as wild as this. How about you, Amelia, my dear sister?"

"I've had adventures around the world and seen the great magicians of France, Egypt, China, and more," Amelia says, "and this . . . this little show was on par with the best of them." She smiles and winks at you.

Blushing, you take a bow. Even though you've just arrived in this world, you feel that this evening has gone beyond your wildest expectations. But this is a game, and all games have some sort of twist. What will this one's twist be?

"Shall we have a refreshment?" asks Professor Carter. "After that astonishment, I'd be surprised if we all weren't in need of something to wet our whistles. What say we—"

Before he can finish his sentence, a voice from everywhere booms out. "ARBADAK ARBA!" it says, and a black cloud appears out of nowhere between you and the trio. It dissipates immediately, revealing none other than your archrival, the nefarious magician Nefario the Infernal!

"So, I heard through the magical grapevine that you were attempting to impress the smart set with your cheap tricks," Nefario says to you, stroking his pointy Van Dyke beard. "Well, the tricks may work if you don't look too closely, but what would the people think if they saw some REAL magic, eh?"

Nefario snaps his fingers, and cages drop from above, coming out of nowhere, trapping each of the three onlookers. They grab the bars, panic on their faces, and another snap drops black cloths over the cages. "Presto-chango," says Nefario, twisting his thin and curling mustache, and with practiced grace and speed, he whips the cloths off the cages one-two-three, revealing that the prisoners have disappeared!

"Ha ha ha ha!" he laughs diabolically. "I present you with this challenge, my rival—search this house for my magical hostages and free them. If you succeed, then we shall know who is the greatest magician in the world. If you fail, I suppose then we'll know who isn't. Ha ha ha ha ha!"

Nefario turns and runs toward the door of the library, and just when it appears as if he's going to collide with it, he gestures and disappears in a flash of darkness and black smoke—smoke that lingers, then twists and turns unnaturally until it dissipates, revealing . . .

MAGICIAN'S GAMBIT

Act 1

THE CURTAIN RISES

. . . and you realize that Nefario the Infernal has vanished and taken your audience with him. They may be in terrible danger.

You're alone in the library of Professor Carter's mansion. Tomes of all kinds line the shelves around you, and a fire burns in the stone fireplace, a fire that you don't recall being lit a second ago, a fire that's going pretty nicely. In fact, it's going a little TOO nicely, as it seems to be growing by the second! Fingers of flame begin to extend from the hearth, snaking out as if they're alive. In moments, the room is ablaze, and the fire is moving to block the library door, the only way out! Soon the entire room will be alight, so you'd better make your escape. It's time to actually play *Magician's Gambit*, so . . .

What's your deal?

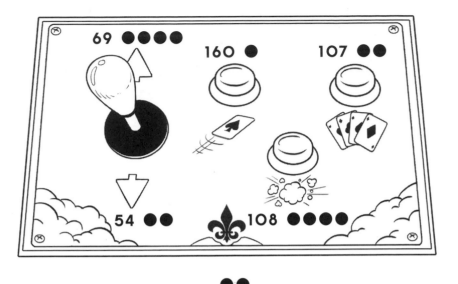

●●

You decide to run around the ring, thinking that maybe you can confuse Gordo. You run around him once. And then twice. And yes, Gordo does look confused. When you're on your third lap around him, though, his look of confusion turns to boredom, and he extends a fist as you pass by, which you run directly into. *BONK!* And ow.

You lie on the floor of the ring, unable to get up, as the rooster referee, Gordo, and Doc (still playing his banjo) stand over you. "Good strategy for a hundred-yard dash, kid," says Doc as you lose consciousness. "Not so good for a boxing match."

YOU'RE KNOCKED OUT.

CONTINUE: Y/N?

Y: Head to 162 ●●   N: Head to 224 ●●

You take the three Devil Cards from your inside jacket pocket and look at the trio of smiling, sinister faces on them. They're certainly interesting, well-made cards, but you're puzzled over what exactly you can DO with them to amaze your expectant audience.

Then, one of the devils on the cards winks at you, followed by the other two! Surprised, you drop the cards, and they flutter to the ground. As you bend down to pick them up, you can hear someone in the audience clear their throat. This is NOT going well.

But before you can collect the cards, something strange begins to happen. The cards move of their own accord, sliding away from your hands and lining up neatly side by side at the foot of the stage. As if this weren't strange enough, a small fire is starting on each card, fires that grow higher and higher until there are three good-size blazes roaring in front of you. Then, suddenly, three figures jump out of the fires and land on the stage—dapper devils dressed in tuxedos and top hats and carrying canes! They each touch their cane to a fire, instantly snuffing the flames, bow to the audience, and pause for a moment, and then they begin to TAP-DANCE, of all things. And not a desultory, bored tap dance. These devils are GOOD, and their energetic, choreographed hoofing soon has the audience hooting and cheering, amazed at their devilish acrobatics.

Then, as suddenly as they began, the devils stop and point their canes at the cards before them. Instantly, flames shoot up. The devils bow again and then leap back into the fires, which flare up momentarily, consuming the demonic dancers, then just as instantly go out completely, leaving the cards completely unscorched. You lean down to pick them up and then throw them to the audience, your aim unerringly finding each of the three in their seats.

"Bravo!" yells Professor Carter.

"Indeed. What a show!" adds Amelia.

"Best. Magician. Ever," concludes Tommy.

Smiling, you take a bow, and you notice that a mist is beginning to whirl around the floor, a theatrical smoke meant to obscure the stage and make everything look more mysterious. But where is it coming from? Whatever its origin, it's getting thicker and thicker, and soon the whole stage is covered in a thick, pea-soup fog so dense that you can't even see a foot ahead of you.

The theater has disappeared, the applause becoming fainter and fainter as another sound replaces it: the sound of arcade games! As the smoke clears, you can see that you're no longer inside *Magician's Gambit*—you've returned to your own world!

If you want to play *Wild Goose Chase!*, head to 205 ●●

If you've completed both games, head to 224 ●●

●●●●

You and Gordo square off again in the middle of the Pig Pen's ring. This time, though, your opponent seems to be cautiously watching you, wary of what you might do. Could it be that you've given him something to think about? Hmm. Maybe? Your next move will be the test of that theory.

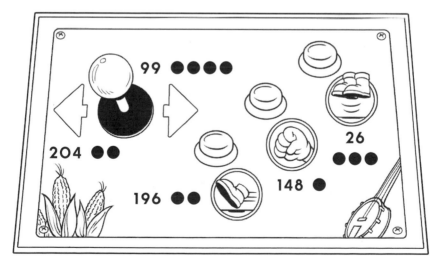

Outside in the hallway, you tentatively reach out a hand toward the library door. The door handle turns easily. It's unlocked. The door opens, and no smoke or flames leap out at you.

You look up and down the beautiful hall; behind you, it comes to a dead end at a large stained-glass window that depicts a scene of a magician in the act of pulling a rabbit out of a hat. Ahead, the hallway extends past doorways until it reaches the house's foyer, where a staircase leads up to its second floor. If you know anything about mysteries and/or video games, you know that you're going to have to climb up the levels of this strange mansion to get to the bottom of this mystery and/or beat the game. So what's your move?

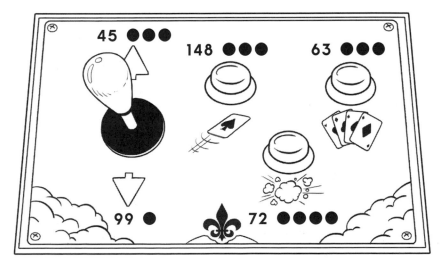

●●

You wait until the very last second . . . and you jam the car's wheel to the right! But the geese have veered to the left, down the other fork! You slam on the brakes and try to turn around, but the jalopy gets stuck in a five-point turn.

"#@%&*!" says Sheriff Farmer in frustration.

Doc is no longer playing the banjo—he's broken a string and is whistling a sad tune.

THAT'S THE END, PEOPLE!
CONTINUE: Y/N?
Y: Head to 183 ●●   N: Head to 224 ●●

●●●

You retreat from the remaining stained-glass rabbits, who stalk you down the hallway but don't seem to want to be shattered by your deadly deck. Then, they suddenly stop, as if they've reached an invisible barrier, turn, and hop away, the sound of clinking glass receding into the darkness of the hall. You turn from them and see that you're almost at the end of the corridor. Ahead of you, you can see the mansion's foyer and the staircase to the second floor, and to both your right and left there are closed doors. From the foyer, you can hear the sounds of a struggle . . . and a scream! From behind the door on your right comes the growling of what sounds like a fearsome beast, and from behind the door on your left, you hear diabolical laughter. Which way do you go?

If you try the door on the left, head to 222 ●
If you go forward, head to 164 ●
If you try the door on the right, head to 186 ●●

●●●●

You press on the accelerator of the car, causing it to zoom forward and gain on the gooses, er, geeses, um, GEESE!

"Good job, Deputy," shouts Sheriff Farmer. "I might have a shot. Don't lose your nerve! Keep on 'em!"

Head to 168 ●●

●

You draw a card from your deck and release it in one swift motion, its deadly arc taking it through the ear of one of the stained-glass rabbits, shattering the appendage into pieces. The rabbits pause and look at you warily, then shake off their fear and advance on you again! Choose another move.

Head back to 146 ●●●

●●

You jump into the seats on your left, and Granny's rolling pin whizzes to the right, just missing you. That was a close one, but as she grabs the rolling pin again, the crooked goose hitches up her bag of money and runs out of the car.

"We'd better follow that goose, kid," says Doc (still

playing his banjo, but faster now). "Let's go!"

Head to 9 ●●●

●●●

You move away from your audience, walking backward, keeping all three gazes locked to yours, as if you're retreating to reveal something. Then you move back to where you were standing previously.

Head back to 89 ●● to try another move, and if you've tried them all, go to 192 ●

●●

You hustle a little to your left, and Gordo cagily moves to the right, keeping you in his sights. That's not going to do it. You both examine each other warily. Try another move.

Head back to 199 ●●●●

●●●●

You back away from Hercules as the rabbit runs toward you but find yourself backing into another door! You desperately try the handle, but it's locked. Choose another move!

Head back to 164 ●

●

You make a motion with your hand, a flourish throwing something at the ground, and when you do, you disappear in a puff of smoke, only to instantaneously reappear halfway up a nearby ladder that leads to the upper shelves of books in the library. Before the looks of shock even begin to register on your audience's faces, you disappear again, reappearing less than a moment later where you started. *This would be an effective way to jump and get to hard-to-reach places*, you think.

Head back to 89 ●● to try another move, and if you've tried them all, head to 192 ●

●●

You find yourself irresistibly drawn to the *Wild Goose Chase!* cabinet. The lighthearted, cartoony art on the side of the game cabinet promises a rural variation on the classic slapstick scenario of cops and robbers, only in this case the cop is a farmer and the robbers are anthropomorphic domesticated (and criminally minded) fowl. And the game's attract mode music—digital bluegrass banjo played at bonkers, escape-velocity speed—makes you wonder if some of the wacky chases that must be in the game end with someone falling into piles of mysterious brown stuff.

Good and whimsical times, you figure, so you stand before the game. The music increases in speed and volume, becoming even more manic. The Midnight Arcade token feels warm between your fingers as you bring it to the coin slot, almost as if it's been lying out in the hot sun. You let it drop, and when you do, the intense music seemingly breaks free from whatever was holding it back, and the banjo gets plucked faster . . . faster . . . faster, until you can barely tell one note from another! All around you, the light gets brighter and brighter, the murky darkness of the arcade rapidly replaced by . . . sunlight? You look behind you: The arcade is disappearing, and suddenly you smell . . . nature. All of it—the earthy aroma of hay, the even earthier scent of cow manure. It smells just like that farm you went to on a field trip last year in school. But how could the arcade smell like a farm? You look at the cabinet again, wondering if you missed something about a gimmick involving "Smell-o-Gaming," but your inspection reveals no hidden vents, nothing. The smells get even stronger, and you hear a voice yell, "Wiiiiilllllllld Goose Chase!" Surprised and weirded out, you let go of the controls and stumble backward. The light gets even brighter, and as you shield your eyes, you lose your footing and tumble to the ground . . .

. . . and find yourself sitting not on the gum-encrusted carpet of the arcade, but on your butt in the grass. You aren't even inside anymore. You look around, blinking in the harsh light of day, and standing up, you take in your surroundings: It's a hot, sunny day wherever you are, and where you are appears to be a small park that makes up the main square of a small town—but it looks like a small town built with the strangest architectural plans available. A road borders the park, and farm buildings like stables, grain silos, and such stand all around the other side of the road, each bearing the name of a business. And straight ahead of you, dominating the town square, is a large building that looks like a barn, but a barn that's been converted into a central meeting place of some sort. Over the open barn doors hangs a sign that reads "Farmingtonville Town Hall and First Agricultural Bank." A set of wide, wooden steps lead up to the barn doors, and people walk in and out, merrily going about their business.

But wait. There's something strange about the people. You squint at them, then widen your eyes.

Those aren't PEOPLE.

They're ANIMALS.

Walking, talking animals! Cows, pigs, dogs, horses, sheep . . . every kind of farm creature you can imagine, all dressed in old-timey clothes that make them look like something out of a vintage cartoon.

Yep. You're on a farm, all right, but it's a WEIRD farm: You're on the farm in *Wild Goose Chase!*

"Afternoon, stranger," says someone near you. Turning, you see that the person speaking is not actually a human person—it's an old hound dog sitting on a bench in the park. He is dressed in a flannel shirt and overalls and has a banjo on his lap, on which he idly picks out a lazy melody. You stare in dumbfounded astonishment, which is what one does the first time one sees a banjo-playing hound. "Well, I take it from your dumbfounded astonishment that you are simply overwhelmed by the beauty and splendor of the surroundings of your new posting. Let me be the first to welcome you to Farmingtonville. Name's Doctor, but everybody round these parts calls me Doc." He extends a paw, and you shake it and say hello, figuring you've already been rude enough.

"You're new in this town, I reckon," Doc says as he absentmindedly strums gentle chords on his banjo. "Well, as you can see, we're a quiet little community, not much happenin'"—Doc looks around suspiciously, like someone might be listening in, and lowers his voice—"'cept of course for the GOOSE CRIME WAVE." His eyes bug out cartoonishly.

Almost as if on cue, a commotion breaks out at the building across the park, a riot of squawking and mayhem! Turning to see what's the matter, you see a pair of birds push their way out of the structure. But these aren't any ordinary birds—they're two geese, one who looks like a mean old grandma, and another who looks like the goose equivalent of a brick wall: big, dumb, and thuggish. The grandma goose carries a rolling pin, which she uses to take out the security guards who chase after her, conking them on their heads as easy as one-two-three. The big bruiser goose carries a load that looks like a pile of money bags.

"Well, I'll be," says Doc, plucking on his banjo, increasing the tempo. "There I was talking about a goose crime wave, and the goose crime wave just plumb and showed up and robbed the town bank. How about that?"

Your jaw wide-open in amazement, you watch as the two crooked fowl run down the steps of the building and into a waiting car, with what can only be described as a weaselly-looking goose at the wheel. The getaway car screeches into motion as soon as the two other geese get in and weaves wildly around the square, almost clobbering a bunch of animals, before it takes off into the streets of the farm city. It's barely gone a second before another car enters the square you're standing in . . . and drives directly toward you and Doc, skidding to a halt next to you. A man—not a walking animal, a goofy-looking human dressed in a combination of farm gear and sheriff duds—gets out and runs up to you and Doc, the old car idling and wheezing behind him.

"Howdy, Sheriff Farmer," says Doc.

"Good to see ya, Doc," says the sheriff, tipping his hat at Doc before turning to you. "I been lookin' all over town for you, Deputy, and here you are, lollygaggin' with Doc in the park while we got some gooses, I mean geeses, I mean GEESE to catch, and I'm deputizing YOU to drive! Get in!" The sheriff jumps back into the car in the passenger seat and pats the driver's seat. "Hop in the back, Doc. We're going to need some chase music!"

Knowing that this must be how the game works—and that's right, you're in a game!—you jump behind the wheel, Doc squeezing into the back seat behind you and playing an easygoing banjo riff as you sit there, idling.

"Well?" the sheriff says, looking at you expectantly. "What are you waiting for, Deputy? Give the controls a try, and let's see how you drive. Then we can chase us some Wild Geese!"

Drive the car? But . . . aha! You remember the controls on the *Wild Goose Chase!* cabinet back in the Midnight Arcade.

You're going to have to think of this as playing a game if you want to get anywhere, so what do you want to do, kid?

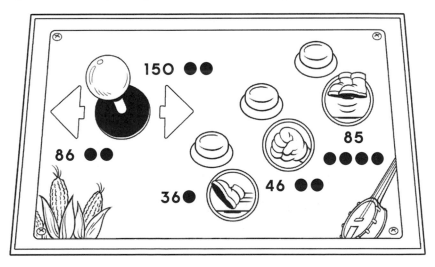

●●●

You got . . .

. . . the Fool Card! Which means you get NOTHING. Fie and alas! But at least you survived your encounter with the mysterious devil magician in the crystal ball. Tossing the useless card back on the table, you turn and see the mirror open behind you.

Head to 14 ●●●

You throw a left, then a right, and then a left again, and with each punch, Doc stops playing the banjo and holds up a paw. *Smack, smack, smack!* Blow after blow connects with a satisfying feeling of impact. Doc shakes both of his paws in mock pain. "Watch it, kid. That there's my frettin' hand, and this here's my pickin' hand. You don't want my banjo-playin' days to be over, do ya? Don't answer that. Anyway, you got some decent power there. Look for the right opening, and then lay into 'em!"

Continue your training and head back to 57 ●●●● **to try another move. If you've tried them all, head to 187** ●●●●

●

You climb the stairs to the second floor of the mansion, a winding set of steps that seems to go on far longer than what is possible in a normal home. The stairs turn and turn and turn, until you can no longer see the first floor. But just like you can't kid a kidder, you can't, er, magic a magician. This must be an illusion of Nefario's, you figure, some sort of ruse to confuse and befuddle you. And if it's an illusion, you know that there's an end to it, somehow.

You continue upward on the stairs, until you finally reach what appears to be their end: The next few steps have rotted and crumbled away, leaving a gap between you and the second-floor landing just ahead. The gap looks like it might be too far to jump, and below, there appears to be nothing except a terribly long fall. But that's strange—Professor Carter's mansion is otherwise impeccably maintained. How could there be something within in such obvious disrepair?

As you ponder this anomaly, your magic senses begin to crackle; something isn't right on these stairs. Your instincts are telling you that you are being followed. You look down the stairwell: There's nothing there, except for steps descending into darkness . . .

. . . a darkness that's gradually getting brighter. And warmer! An orange glow is swiftly approaching, the stairwell is getting so hot that you begin to sweat in your tuxedo, and the reason is quickly apparent—the stairwell is on fire, and the fire is spreading toward you, consuming the steps furiously! In the flames, you can just barely make out a face, then another, and another, before they shift and disappear—they're all the grinning face of Nefario!

Just across the seemingly impossible gap is the landing of the next floor. You're almost there, but you're presented with a seemingly impossible choice: keep going forward and perhaps fall into oblivion, or try your luck on the stairs, against the fire.

What's your play, magician?

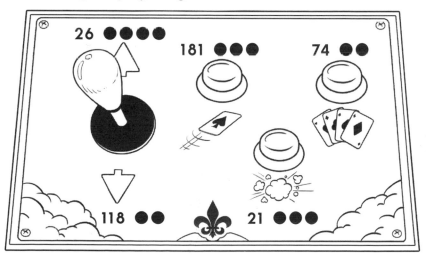

●●

You're coming up to a Farmingtonville intersection, where the road forks to the left and the right. The geese's car is disabled, with one of its back tires flapping around and tattered, but it's still managing to pull away from you. It bobs back and forth, like it could go either way, so you'd better follow closely!

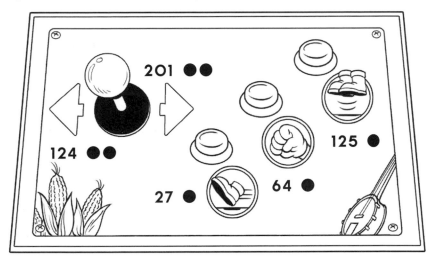

●●●

You pull a pair of Devil Cards from your pocket, holding one in each hand to display them for your captive audience, but they don't know that you're stalling for time, trying to figure out what to do next.

That decision is taken out of your hands, literally, when the two cards begin to shake and twist of their own accord, almost as if they're trying to free themselves from your grasp. You hold on to them at first, out of instinct, and the Devil Cards writhe with a strength that you wouldn't expect a playing card to have. Your attempt to maintain your grip becomes a struggle, and the cards pull your arms this way and that. To the audience it must look like some sort of sophisticated mime act, for they laugh and clap as the cards pull you from one end of the stage to the other. Finally, you can take no more and release the cards, but instead of following the law of gravity and falling to the ground, the cards float in the air for a moment. You and your audience both stare at them, all of you wondering what's going to happen next. Then, an invisible force begins to fold the cards as they dangle there, unseen fingers manipulating them until, moments later, they have a new shape: They've become elaborate origami dragons! The miniature card-dragons flap their wings and then begin to circle your body, breathing fire from their little mouths. You realize that the magical creatures will follow the motions of your hands, and soon you are orchestrating their flight around the stage and then over the heads of your audience, the minor movements of your fingers causing the card-dragons to loop and twirl acrobatically and the audience to gasp in delight.

Then, sensing it's time for a finale, inspiration strikes, and you decide to lace your fingers together. You don't know what's going to happen, but the results are spectacular: The card-dragons begin to stream fire at each other, battling with flames, and soon both of them have ignited and are rapidly consumed by their infernos. The ashes of the cards rain down on the audience, which claps wildly and appreciatively.

But you notice that the smoke from the card-dragons' immolation hasn't dissipated. In fact, it's getting thicker, filling the theater like a fog until you can no longer see beyond the footlights at the edge of the stage. Soon, the theater has disappeared, the applause becoming fainter and fainter as another sound replaces it: the sound of arcade games! As the smoke clears, you can see that you're no longer inside *Magician's Gambit*—you've returned to your own world!

If you want to play *Wild Goose Chase!*, head to 205 ●●

If you've completed both games, head to 224 ●●

The old car roars to life and skids out of the park, heading in the general direction of the fleeing Goose Gang. You hang on to the wheel, making sure that you don't run into anything or crash into one of the weird farm city buildings to either side of you. Okay, it's definitely that sort of game so far—you don't have to make the car go, just make sure the car doesn't go somewhere it's not supposed to go. Got it? Easy, right?

"Here's the skinny, kid," the sheriff continues as the car skids around a corner, leading you farther into the farm city. He's pulled what looks like an old-timey machine gun from under his seat, but he's also got a . . . bag of potatoes? You get even more confused when he begins to load the gun WITH potatoes!

"What?" he says. "You've never seen a SPUD GUN before?" Finished loading, he says, "You and me, we are the law, sworn protectors and keepers of the peace of Farmingtonville. That Goose Gang we're going after"— he points out the windshield, and farther ahead, you can see the getaway car weaving around the road, shooting out smoke and sparks and all manner of cartoonlike stuff—"they're public enemies number one, two, and three. You gonna help me nab 'em?"

You nod nervously, trying to keep your eyes on the road.

"Okay then. Let's get 'em! You drive, I'll shoot!"

And with that, Sheriff Farmer crawls out the window to stand on the running board of the car, his Spud Gun in hand.

"I only have two rules, kid: Don't knock me off, and don't crash!" he yells.

Gulp.

Your old jalopy is careening through the mean streets of Farmingtonville, in hot pursuit of a carload of criminal-minded gooses. Or is it geeses? No, it's GEESE (we think)! Anyway, the car is steadily getting farther and farther away. What do you do?

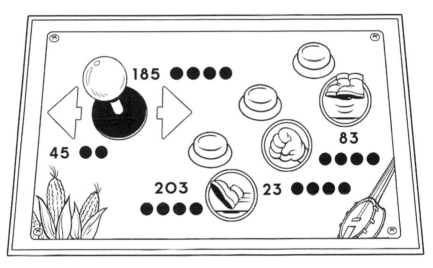

You turn the knob on the door on the left, and it springs open, revealing a small, dark room. You enter, and the door closes behind you in an instant. Turning to try to get out, you cannot find a doorknob, a latch, anything! The wall is entirely smooth. Mist gathers around your ankles, swirling lazily.

Turning back around, you see that in the middle of the room is a small round table, at which sits a strange

person. They're dressed in a tuxedo similar to yours, but it's unnaturally shiny, and you can't see their face, for they're wearing a mask that resembles nothing less than a devil—horns, crafty eyes, grinning mouth, and fancy goatee. They gesture with their hand, inviting you to sit in the seat before them. Intrigued, you do, and once you're seated, the mysterious devil takes a deck of cards from the table and begins to shuffle them in crazy, acrobatic ways. Cards fly to and fro, and you're amazed by the sheer skill involved. Finally, the cards apparently shuffled to their satisfaction, the devil deals three cards onto the table, facedown. It's a trick of some sort! You reach out to touch one, and the devil holds up a finger of warning and begins to speak.

"Be careful," the devil says, their sinister voice sending chills down your spine. "One of these cards will bring you certain death, another will bring you nothing, but one will eventually show you great wonder and bring you great delight. You have a choice: Pick a card, or leave the way you came."

The devil spreads their hands. The choice is up to you!

If you decide to skip choosing a card and leave the room, go to 164 ●

If you choose to pick a card, head to 149 ● ● ●

To your surprise, you find yourself back in the real world, but you're no longer inside the Midnight Arcade—you're just outside of Cats Waller's Backstage Game Room, and this time there's a locked gate blocking the way, a gate that you know for certain wasn't there before. What the . . . ?

Next to you, Cats Waller and His Sarsaparilla Syncopators are losing steam, coming to the end of what sounds like some sort of ragtime tune, but one played by old animatronic puppet musicians that haven't been serviced in decades. It's slow and freaky, and after a moment all four members in the quartet slow down to stillness, and the music stops completely. All is quiet, both inside the Olde Tymes Pizza Parlour and inside the game room. Peering through the gate, you see all the games that you THOUGHT were on and working covered by dusty plastic sheeting. It looks like the games haven't been used in years.

And maybe they haven't. Maybe you had some sort of weird episode and imagined everything that just happened. Or "happened." Yeah, that's it. Otherwise, it's impossible.

You leave the Olde Tymes Pizza Parlour and make your

way through the maze of corridors that brought you there, finally finding the restroom and making a quick stop before you head back to your family.

When you return to their table, you apologize to your parents for being gone so long, and when you do, they both look at you quizzically.

"What do you mean?" asks your mom. "You went potty—excuse me—went to the restroom, right? You left and came right back. What's to apologize for?"

Came right back? But you know you've been gone for at least an hour. This is so confusing, and the level of noise of all the fun being had in the Extreme Party Zone isn't helping at all. You shake your head and absentmindedly put your hand in the pocket of your hoodie, looking for something to fidget with. Your hand touches two things, and you take them out of your pocket and look at them, shocked.

One of the items is a golden coin, a game token that says "MA" on one side.

The other item is a playing card with a familiar-looking back. On the other side of the card—it's a joker—there's a picture of someone you recognize: the attendant of the Midnight Arcade! But . . . how?

All of a sudden, you feel hot, flustered. You unzip your hoodie to get some air, and your other mom's eyebrows raise with surprise.

"Hey, is that a new shirt? It's cool," she says.

A new shirt? What? "No," you respond, looking down, "it's the same old—"

But it's not. You know for a fact that this morning you put on an old T-shirt, not caring what you wore to the party, but somehow, someway, you aren't wearing it anymore.

Instead, you're wearing a shirt just like the attendant's, a baseball T-shirt with a retro logo across the front: the logo of the Midnight Arcade!

ABOUT THE AUTHOR

Known for the popular online role-playing game *Sword & Backpack*, Gabe Soria has written several books for Penguin Young Readers, including *Regular Show's Fakespeare in the Park* and Shovel Knight's *Digger's Diary*. He has written several comic books for DC Comics, including Batman '66. Gabe also collaborated with friend Dan Auerbach of the Black Keys on the *Murder Ballads* comic book. He lives in New Orleans, Louisiana.

ABOUT THE ILLUSTRATOR

Kendall Hale is a cartoonist from Wisconsin whose work has varied from animated character designs to commercial advertising. He has produced work for Nick Jr., Bento Box, Skippy Peanut Butter, and Sandman Studios. He has also taught classes at Brigham Young University. He currently lives in Los Angeles, California, with his pet rock, Rock.

This one's for Charlie, Rob, and Karl, 'cause they give me extra lives—GS

W

PENGUIN WORKSHOP

An Imprint of Penguin Random House LLC, New York

Text copyright © 2019 by Gabe Soria. Illustrations copyright © 2019 by Kendall Hale. All rights reserved. Published by Penguin Workshop, an imprint of Penguin Random House LLC, New York. PENGUIN and PENGUIN WORKSHOP are trademarks of Penguin Books Ltd, and the W colophon is a registered trademark of Penguin Random House LLC. Printed in the USA.

Visit us online at www.penguinrandomhouse.com.

Library of Congress Cataloging-in-Publication Data is available upon request.

ISBN 9781524784355

10 9 8 7 6 5 4 3 2 1